MURDER BY LETHAL INJECTION

PAULA BERNSTEIN

M&Z PRESS

To Sheri and Pam,
Who are always there for me.

I T WAS THREE O'CLOCK IN THE MORNING AND I WAS drenched in blood. It had spattered uncontrollably over my shirt, dripped down my pants, and soaked through the thick white socks I'd worn under my rubber-soled sandals. I eyed myself with distaste. The fluorescent light in the deserted women's locker room gave a sallow cast to my light skin and emphasized the dark circles under my green eyes. I wondered if I was getting too old to keep doing this.

I removed the bloody scrubs and tossed them into the laundry bin. There were stains on my new, peach lace, Lily of France brassiere. I stepped out of my underwear, wrapped myself in two skimpy hospital towels, turned on the shower and retrieved the shampoo and conditioner I kept in my locker for nights like this. The hot water felt soothing and reminded me of how exhausted I was.

Strictly speaking, I didn't even have to be here. Ruth, my partner, was on call this weekend and for the rest of my well-earned week of vacation. But when Esther Lieberman had gone into labor with her sixth child that morning, I couldn't bring myself to leave. I'd taken care of Esther since her marriage at the age of eighteen and had delivered all of her previous children. She held the record in my practice for the largest number of births and considered me her good luck charm. She swore she couldn't have a baby without me. For my part, I'd always considered her one of my favorite patients, and besides, how long could a sixth baby take?

Unfortunately, it had taken fourteen hours and had resulted in a bouncing ten-and-a-half pound baby boy, followed by a massive postpartum hemorrhage. I'd massaged Esther's uterus, given her a shot of prostaglandin and a lot of IV fluid, and had stayed with her for over an hour, just to be certain she was really stable and wasn't going to hemorrhage again.

I dried off, ran a comb through the tangles of my curly red hair, stuffed my bloody underwear into my giant purse, and put a clean set of scrubs on over my braless, middle-aged body. I doubted anyone would notice, and I didn't have the energy to get back into my office clothes for the fifteen-minute drive from Los Angeles Memorial Hospital to my Brentwood condominium.

The physician's parking lot was deserted at this hour. Only two other cars, besides my own, bore witness to the hours doctors keep. I could feel my heart starting to pound as I looked for intruders lurking in corners, and car key in hand, achieved the safety of my locked vehicle. Why hadn't I thought about calling hospital security to escort me to my car? Just a few weeks ago, one of my colleagues had been mugged in this very spot. Another had been shot and almost killed in his driveway by thugs who had followed him home from the hospital after a delivery. I, of all people, knew that no one was safe from the escalating crime wave that had hit Los Angeles in recent years. I'd had far too much experience with crime close to home.

It had been a little over a year since my life was shattered, for the second time, by death. The first loss was my beloved husband, Ben, who passed away five years ago, shortly before the birth of our daughter Zoe. Last year, I'd dealt with the violent murder of my sister-in-law, Beth. I had been devastated and obsessed by her death, functioning like an automaton and spending all my spare time and energy searching her past rather than attempting to get on with my own present. Daniel Ross had been the investigating officer on her case and it had been a combination of his patience and kindness, along with the final conviction of Beth's killer, that had allowed me to finally begin to let go. Just a few months ago, Daniel and I had become lovers, and we were leaving together in the morning for a well-earned, and badly needed, joint vacation.

I pulled out of the parking lot and headed for Brentwood, glancing frequently in my rearview mirror to be certain no one was following. When I reached home, everything seemed quiet. I could hear Emilia, my housekeeper, snoring gently on the fold-out sofa in the den. She didn't live with us full-time any longer, but she always made herself available to stay with my daughter Zoe when I was on call or had to go out of town. I tiptoed through the living room, careful not to wake Emilia, and up the carpeted stairway to my bedroom.

The room smelled of lemon oil and fresh laundry, with an overlay of night jasmine wafting in through the open window. I turned on the soft light of the Tiffany reproduction lamp on my bedside table. The bed had been made with my favorite cream-colored Egyptian cotton sheets and piles of fluffy, large, decorative pillows. The down comforter was turned invitingly down. The wood on my antique

French desk, the one my late husband Ben and I had found on our honeymoon, gleamed in the soft light.

With a sigh of contentment, I shed my clothes, set my alarm for six-thirty so I wouldn't miss my plane the next morning, and crawled under the covers. Within minutes I was sound asleep.

Daniel arrived promptly at seven a.m. to drive us both to the airport, and I heard Emilia let him in. I was still in the process of getting dressed and putting on enough make-up so that I didn't look half dead.

"Hurry up, Hannah," Daniel called from downstairs.

"Okay, okay." I searched my voluminous carry-on, one more time, to be certain I'd remembered everything: tickets, itinerary, reservations, make-up, hair dryer, sunscreen, iPad, antacids, smart phone, chargers and beeper. After some consideration, I removed my beeper. Where we were going, I wasn't supposed to need it. Daniel thought I'd lost my marbles when I'd completed all my vacation packing a week ahead of time, but I'd known better. In my line of work, you could never count on having time when you needed it. Finally, dragging my luggage, I made an appearance.

"Have a great trip, Mommy." Zoe, my adorable five-year-old, reached up for another hug and I almost cancelled the reservations.

I hadn't gone anywhere without her since she was born and I was feeling a little guilty about leaving her behind. But, I had explained that Daniel and I were going somewhere that would be pretty boring for kids, and that she couldn't miss school, and she had seemed okay with it.

"We'll be just fine. Don't worry," said Emilia.

"Remember," I said. "She is not allowed to eat at McDonald's every night while I'm away."

"I won't, Mommy. I'll have pizza too," Zoe said.

"Great. That really eases my mind."

Daniel bent down and planted a kiss on Zoe's cheek. "Don't worry, Princess. I'll take good care of your mother."

"I'm not a princess, I'm a Ninja Turtle," Zoe said.

"Cowabunga, dude," Daniel said, assuming a karate stance.

Zoe reached for the nearest weapon and backed him into a far corner of the living room. "Take that, Shred Head."

I kept a careful eye on my contemporary art glass collection. Zoe knew better than to damage it, but I had some trepidation about Daniel.

"I'm ready," I announced.

Daniel extricated himself and lifted my suitcase. "Boy, are you lucky I work out."

I just smiled and opened the front door.

CHAPTER TWO

A S IT TURNED OUT, WE GOT TO THE AIRPORT IN plenty of time. I settled myself comfortably in the window seat, with a cup of coffee and my e-book. Daniel ordered orange juice, then leaned over and dropped a kiss on my forehead. I'd only had two significant relationships in my life: Ben, my husband, and Daniel, who had helped me end a five-year period of celibacy after Ben's death. Our romantic relationship was still pretty new and I wasn't sure where it was headed, but for the moment, I was just grateful to have him beside me.

I'd actually initiated the vacation for two when I realized how emotionally depleted I was. My feelings for Daniel were a combination of warmth, gratitude and a sexual attraction powerful enough to occupy my fantasy life every waking moment. I daydreamed about him when I drove to the hospital every morning, imagined his hands on me when I sat in my consultation room between patients, and forced away memories of our lovemaking when I had to concentrate in the operating room. My brain was still cautious about this new relationship, but my body was not ambivalent.

I was smart enough to realize that if I wanted to nurture this relationship, Daniel and I needed some quality time together, uninterrupted by the demands of work and of my beloved daughter, who had first priority in my life. To accomplish this, I announced to him that I desperately needed a beach, sunshine, a mystery novel and good company, not necessarily in that order. He'd arrived at my house that same evening, loaded with travel information.

We'd settled on an island called Marianne's Key, off the coast of South Carolina. Among the locals, the island was a popular honeymoon destination because there was nothing to do there, other than lie supine on the beach or in the bedroom. The concept appealed to me.

We landed at Charleston, only ten minutes behind schedule, and rented a small American car with a giant air conditioner. The temperature was about eighty-five degrees, with humidity to match, and it was only the beginning of May. My red hair, which usually hangs halfway down my back, frizzed to shoulder length and my sunglasses fogged.

"Don't worry," Daniel said, as he rubbed a thumb over my lenses. "It's not like this at the beach."

"I'm counting on that," I said.

We meandered our way up I-95, in the direction of Beaufort, where the ferry was. We made it a few minutes early, bought our tickets, and drove the rental car onto the lower deck.

The sun was just setting as the ferry took off. The clouds over the shore had a rosy glow, the water lapped quietly at the prow of the ship, and a soft, salt-laden breeze promised a cooler evening. I leaned against the rail, watching the lights come on in Beaufort.

Daniel stood behind me, slipping his arms around my shoulders. "Is it starting to feel like you're on vacation yet?"

I shifted my weight and relaxed against his chest. "Pretty close."

We watched in silence for a while longer, until I started to get chilly. Then we went inside, ordered two cups of hot chocolate, and kept an eye out for signs of the island.

It took about half an hour to get to Marianne's Key, a long, flat island that appeared to be forested on the leeward side. We caught a glimpse of lights through the trees and then the ferry pulled up at a long, wooden jetty. We disembarked and drove our car onto the island's only road.

We were staying at the Sandpiper Inn, once an original Vanderbilt cottage. According to the brochures, it contained twenty bedrooms, each with its own bathroom, a full-service dining room specializing in southern cuisine, and a private beach. We found it at the southern tip of the island; a large house of weathered wood, with one of those wrap-around porches that seem to be a mainstay of southern architecture. I could see several rope hammocks suspended from the porch ceiling.

We rang the bell, and receiving no response, tried the front door. We entered a large hallway, where a curved staircase with an elaborately carved mahogany banister led to the second story. To the right, was a parlor with a marble fireplace, an oriental rug and a profusion of English antique furnishings. To the left, was a dining room with a mahogany table, exquisitely set for twenty, with Wedgwood china and cut crystal.

"I'm not sure I can eat here," I said to Daniel. "I'd be afraid of breaking the antique china."

"Oh, we don't eat here. That's the Vanderbuilts' original dining room. The guest dining room is in back."

I turned, and found myself face-to-face with a smiling elderly lady. She had teased gray hair, and was wearing a frilly pink blouse with pearl buttons and a white apron.

"You must be the Rosses. I'm Mrs. Smithers, the housekeeper. Let me show you to your room. Charlie will bring up your luggage."

Charlie was apparently the surly-looking teenager standing behind her.

I didn't bother to correct her misapprehension. I found it difficult to tell someone my mother's age that I was traveling with a man I wasn't married to, and besides, it was none of her business. We followed her upstairs.

"Your room looks directly out at the beach," she said, opening the door to a large bedroom.

Pale green carpet covered the floor. Green and white sprigged wallpaper, with matching drapes, covered the walls. A mahogany four-poster bed, with a white eyelet cotton canopy and comforter, stood in the center. French doors led out to the second-floor balcony. I stood outside for a moment and listened. It was too dark to see the ocean but I could hear the waves breaking against the dunes.

"It's lovely," I said.

"Dinner's from seven to nine-thirty. The dining room's in the back. Just follow the hallway at the foot of the stairs."

"Are you busy this time of year?" Daniel asked.

Mrs. Smithers shook her head. "The season doesn't begin until mid-June. We're full on the weekends but there are only two other couples staying here now."

Charlie brought up our suitcases and deposited them on the floor. Daniel handed him a tip and Charlie flashed us a grin as he escorted Mrs. Smithers out of the room.

"Private enough for you?" Daniel asked.

"As long as we don't have to talk to the two other couples."

"I'll try and arrange that." Daniel drew me into his arms and started to kiss me.

I felt a sharp stab of desire and eyed the four-poster. On second thought, wonderful smells were emanating from the kitchen and I was famished. I always made passionate love better on a full stomach.

"Do you think we should change before dinner?" I murmured.

"Probably." Daniel released me and lifted both suitcases to the bed. "You'd better change in the bathroom. If I see you without any clothes on, we'll never make it to dinner."

CHAPTER THREE

DINNER WAS SERVED IN A CHARMING ROOM THAT was part indoors and part screened-in back porch. French doors divided it in half and could be closed in unpleasant weather. A young waitress greeted us at the door and showed us to an outside table. There was a warm breeze, laden with the scent of orange blossoms. The dining room was empty when we got there, the evidence suggesting that the other two couples had eaten and left. I spotted one of them taking a stroll down toward the beach. There was something vaguely familiar about the man.

Daniel looked through the wine list and ordered a bottle of Sauvignon Blanc. The waitress brought it, along with a basket of hush puppies and biscuits. There wasn't any menu.

We clinked our glasses and waited to be served, savoring the cold taste of white wine in our mouths. I wondered what it would be like to spend a whole night with Daniel. Up to now, I'd been unwilling to do that. I couldn't stay at his place, leaving Zoe alone, and I was uncomfortable with the idea of my daughter finding him in my bed in the morning. I had no idea if Daniel was going to wind up as my second husband, or if he'd be only the first in a series of relationships with men that would lead nowhere. I was both pleased and concerned about the fact that Zoe had become attached to him. I didn't want her to get hurt if things didn't work out.

The waitress arrived, bearing two huge plates of king crab legs with fluffy mashed potatoes and tubs of melted butter. She put a bucket on the floor between us for the shells and handed us two bibs. I cracked a leg between my fingers and dipped it in the butter. The sweet white meat dissolved in my mouth and butter dripped down my chin. Eventually, I gave up on my napkin. Dessert was a dense chocolate mousse, rich to excess, even for a chocoholic like myself.

After dinner, we slipped our arms around one other and braved the stairs to our bedroom. I was feeling sated, relaxed, and completely happy for the first time in over a year. Daniel opened the door and kissed me as soon as it closed. Only one of my appetites was truly sated. The other was ready for more.

I woke late the next morning, in a shaft of sunlight that illuminated the sheer white canopy of the four- poster. The shower was running in the bathroom. I rolled over and stretched, luxuriating in the feel of the soft cotton sheets against my body. I was surprised at how rested I felt.

I had been significantly worried that all the romance in my affair with Daniel would evaporate if I discovered that he snored or thrashed around during the night. Fortunately, neither seemed to be the case, although our mutual sleep habits still needed a little negotiation. Daniel was a cuddler. I kept waking up to find him wrapped around me and found myself afraid to move for fear of disturbing him. It took me until at least two a.m. to realize that I could roll him over without his even noticing. After that, I must have slept like the dead, because I was feeling great.

Daniel came out of the bathroom looking irresistible, in white cotton shorts and no T-shirt. Looking at him never failed to take my breath away. His body was fit and tan. He had curly dark hair with a touch of gray, blue eyes with laugh lines at the corners, and sharp cheekbones on a narrow face, with a gentle mouth. His eyes, as he caught my glance, were mesmerizing. I debated the merits of not getting out of bed.

"Come on, Sleeping Beauty. The dining room closes for breakfast in half an hour." Daniel pulled the covers off me and extended a hand.

"I'll be ready in five minutes," I said.

"It is constitutionally impossible for any woman to be ready in five minutes."

I can never resist a challenge, so I looked at my watch. I took a two-minute shower, twisted my hair into a bun, slathered sun block all over, and slipped into a bathing suit and a coverall: four minutes, twenty-three seconds.

This time, the dining room wasn't empty. We sat down, ordered waffles, coffee, ham and eggs, and made our plans for the day. Those consisted primarily of debating how long we could safely lie in the sun and deciding which novels to start first.

"Hannah?" A male voice said from behind my left shoulder.

I turned. The man who was standing behind me was

over six-feet tall and suntanned. Once dark hair, now liberally sprinkled with gray, brushed his collar and receded precipitously from what used to be his hairline. A luxuriant mustache compensated for losing the battle with baldness. Wire-rimmed, round glasses perched on his nose, and a heavy, gold-link bracelet adorned the hand he extended in my direction.

For a moment, I didn't recognize him.

"Wesley?" I said, accepting the hand.

He smiled.

So much for my lovely vacation.

"Daniel, this is an old acquaintance of mine, Dr. Wesley Templeton. Wesley, my friend, Daniel Ross."

"It's been too long, Hannah," Wesley said. "What an extraordinary coincidence running into you here."

There was something almost feral about his smile and I wondered how long he was staying here.

"Let me introduce you to my wife." He motioned to a woman seated at the next table and she rose to join us.

She was tall, at least five-foot-ten, with one of those lean, flat-chested bodies you see in runners. Her face was long and horsey, with prominent teeth, a square jaw and olive skin. Black hair was pulled back into a short ponytail.

"My wife, Erica," Wesley said. He slipped an arm around her shoulders. "Darling, meet Hannah Kline and her friend Daniel Ross. I've known Hannah since medical school."

"Oh," she said. "Are you a nurse?"

"No," I said. "Are you?"

"Hannah was a year ahead of me at Harvard," Wesley said.

She offered a thin smile. "Pediatrics?"

"Obstetrics and Gynecology."

"How interesting," Erica said, managing to look completely bored. "Well, it's nice to meet you both. I hope we'll see you on the beach later today."

It was a large island. Hopefully, we could avoid that less than enchanting prospect.

CHAPTER FOUR

"Old boyfriend?" Daniel asked, as soon as they'd left the room. "Should I start getting jealous?"

I grinned. "What makes you think he's an old boyfriend?"

"Your mouth looked like you'd accidentally swallowed a whole lemon."

"Sloppy detective work, lieutenant. You've just been introduced to a genuine Beverly Hills plastic surgeon. He used to be married to my old Vassar roommate, Sara Hellman. Revolting divorce, about five years ago. I'll spare you the details."

"And the new wife?"

"The old bimbo apparently. I gather he actually married the other woman."

"Sounds interesting," Daniel said. "Are you going to tell me about him?"

What could I tell him about Wesley Templeton? The first thing, I suppose, is that I met him at Harvard. Ben had introduced me. They'd known one another from Yale.

We'd been lunching at a deli in Harvard Square. That was in the days before I started worrying about my cholesterol. Ben, who had his mouth full and was trying to educate me on the finer points of art nouveau architecture, spotted Wesley and waved him over to join us.

The first thing that struck me about him was his good looks. Wesley had piercing blue eyes, a strong jaw, and a shock of thick, sable hair. If I hadn't been head-over-heels about Ben, I confess I'd have been interested. He had that kind of magnetism.

"Hannah, meet Wesley Templeton, if you haven't already. Wesley's a year behind you at the med school." Ben mumbled most of this adroit introduction through the remainder of his roast beef sandwich, and finally managed to clear his diction with a swallow of Coke.

"My pleasure." Wesley smiled at me and extended a hand.

Ben motioned him to sit down. "You're welcome to join us if you're not meeting anyone."

"Thanks," Wesley said. "I'm starved. I just finished dissecting my first cadaver. It was incredible. I never appreciated what an exquisitely designed mechanism the human body is. We worked through every vessel and nerve, identified every muscle. It was like discovering a work of art."

I couldn't imagine how anyone could be hungry after that but I restrained my comments while he ordered. I remembered my first cadaver quite well. I'd named him Harry, in honor of my senior thesis advisor at Vassar, and had fits of coughing from breathing the formalin, every time I got within five feet of him.

"It sounds like you're enjoying med school so far," Ben said.

"I am. It's the most intellectually fascinating material I've ever studied."

I had to agree with that, although my intellectual enthusiasm for medicine was somewhat dampened by the necessity of memorizing and regurgitating an innumerable number of facts which, I was certain, I would never retain past the exams for which they were intended.

"I'm sure it is," Ben said. "But, personally, I could skip the dead body."

"There are unpleasant aspects to every field," Wesley said, with a shrug. "You just block them out and get past them, or better still, learn to appreciate the fact that they can be interesting even if they are unpleasant."

"If you'll excuse me," Ben said, "I need to make room for more Coke."

He got up and headed in the direction of the men's room, leaving me momentarily alone with Wesley.

"So, are you and Ben an item, or just friends?" He asked, his smile quite dazzling.

"We've been dating for several months," I replied.

"You wouldn't happen to have a friend as attractive as you are?"

"Not enough women in the first-year class at the med school?"

"None that have made me fall in love at first sight."

I did a rapid mental survey of my friends, imagining each of them on his elegant arm.

"You might like my old roommate from Vassar," I finally said. "Sara's doing a Ph.D. in clinical psychology here. She's very sweet and quite attractive. If you like, I'll ask her if she's free."

"That's very kind of you, Hannah." Wesley scribbled his phone number on a scrap of paper and passed it to me. "If she's willing to meet me, just give me a call. I'm sure I'd enjoy going out with a friend of yours."

I slipped the scrap of paper into my purse, making a mental note to phone Sara that evening.

"I was the one who fixed Wesley up with Sara," I told Daniel. "Up until a few years ago, I thought it was my best fix-up ever. I guess I'm not a good judge of character. The divorce story is pretty harrowing, definitely not a tale for a romantic vacation."

Daniel laughed. "We'll just avoid them," he said.

After breakfast, Daniel and I packed a beach bag and set out to explore the island. The windward side was a sparkling white beach that seemed to stretch on forever. Gentle sand dunes climbed to a ridge, behind which the island homes nestled. The houses were large, secluded and spaced far apart. A number of them had been converted to small inns but others remained the summerhouses of the well to do. The ocean was a delight, especially for someone used to Southern California waters. The Pacific, near Los Angeles, is cold, rough and full of seaweed. Great for surfing and unpleasant for swimming. Here, warm sea and gentle waves promised perfection.

The entire stretch of beach appeared empty, as far as my eye could see. Perhaps the Templetons had opted for the other side of the island. We found a niche between two dunes and settled in. Daniel went for a run and I curled up with a book, carefully perching my straw hat on my head as freckle protection.

CHAPTER FIVE

D ANIEL TOOK OFF, RUNNING ALONG THE BEACH AT the high tide line. The sand was just firm enough for his running shoes, and a soft ocean breeze kept him from sweating too much in the humid air. He loved beach runs, mostly because at the end, he could cool off with a leisurely swim. He settled into a comfortable pace, glancing back once to where Hannah, in a black, one-piece bathing suit and a large straw hat, sat reading on a low beach chair. God, she was sexy. He loved her warmth and responsiveness in bed, and the gusto with which she embraced all the sensual pleasures, including great food. He imagined her licking a chocolate ice cream cone with absolute concentration. What a contrast to his ex-wife Annie.

He maintained a cordial friendship with Annie after their divorce three years ago. She was a nice woman, and in all fairness, marriage to a police detective wasn't what she'd signed up for. Annie thought she was marrying a corporate lawyer, with the lifestyle that accompanied the profession. She was less than supportive when he decided he hated law and joined the LAPD. She had never gotten used to a life where midnight phone calls took him away for days, and social plans could be disrupted at a moment's notice. Hannah, on the other hand, was an obstetrician. Middle-of-the-night calls were her stock-in-trade, and she always understood when he had to cancel a date, at the last minute, to follow a lead in one of his cases. He was equally unperturbed when a patient in labor disrupted a dinner. He loved her independence and the undemanding way she enjoyed his company.

He fervently hoped that dating her didn't turn out to be a big mistake. He never became involved with women he met during a murder investigation. Murder was a poor prelude to romance. He didn't want his presence to trigger painful memories of Beth's death. But somehow, they seemed to have gotten past that issue. There was something to be said for intense sexual chemistry.

The biggest obstacle now seemed to be Ben, Hannah's deceased husband. Hannah had adored him and Ben was a hard act to follow. Daniel still wondered if having sex with him made her feel unfaithful to Ben's memory. She certainly hadn't acted that way last night. He grinned just thinking about it.

Up ahead, the smooth sand beach became rocky and he slowed his pace to a cool-down walk. He noticed Wesley Templeton picking his way through the rocks, walking in his direction. Daniel wasn't in the mood for a polite chat. He took off his running shoes and socks, left them above the high tide line, and plunged into the warm surf.

I must have dozed off because when I awoke, I was in shadow.

Wesley Templeton was standing over me. "I couldn't decide if I should wake you to say hello. You looked so peaceful."

I scanned the beach quickly. Neither Daniel nor Erica was in sight.

"Out for a walk?" I asked, with as much politeness as I could muster.

He nodded. "I confess, I was hoping to run into you. Are you in touch with Sara?"

"Not for quite a few years. We lost touch, shortly after your divorce."

"I take it you and Ben are no longer together." He said it with what seemed like a smirk of satisfaction, as if I couldn't possibly criticize him if my own marriage had failed.

"Not for the past five years," I said, deciding to skip the details.

"I'm sorry to hear that. I always thought you were an ideally suited couple."

"I'd have said the same about you and Sara. Just goes to show you that you can never know the truth about anyone else's marriage."

"I'm sure she told you her side of what happened. She told every mutual friend we had. They all think I'm a shit."

I shrugged. This turn in the conversation was making me uncomfortable. I was completely uninterested in hearing his side.

"You have no idea how difficult it was to live with Sara. She was chronically depressed all the time, in and out of treatment, completely dysfunctional. I tried to help her. I really did. But I just couldn't handle it anymore."

It sounded so reasonable I'd have almost fallen for it, if I hadn't been the recipient of more confidences from Sara over the years than I'd wanted to hear. It wasn't surprising she'd been chronically depressed. He was a shit.

"You don't have to justify yourself to me, Wesley. It's not my job to judge you."

He gave me one of his more charming smiles. "I know that, but you and Ben were such good friends for such a long time. Anyway, Erica and I are leaving today. I'm still in practice in Beverly Hills, if you'd like to get in touch, or if you need anything."

He eyed my thighs and my jaw line, as if he were evaluating a pre-op.

"Thanks, Wesley. Nice running into you," I said.

I spotted Daniel at the far end of the beach jogging in my direction. Wesley took off with a wave. I got up, doffed my hat, and submerged myself in the ocean. Talking to Wesley had left me feeling dirty.

CHAPTER SIX

"I'm not sure I want to take you home tomorrow," Daniel said, nuzzling his nose into a corner of my neck. "I'm seriously considering kidnapping you and forcing you to vacation with me for the next year."

We were on the leeward side of the island, watching the sunset over the Carolina coast.

"Only a year?" I asked. "Don't tempt me. At the moment, I wouldn't mind picking up Zoe, retiring from medicine and escaping to the South Seas."

"What's stopping you?"

"Kindergarten tuition, and the fact that Ruth would have a nervous breakdown if she had no one to share call with."

Daniel grinned and hugged me. "It's always something."

"It's a nice fantasy, though. It's been a lovely week. You made it really special." I reached up and planted a kiss on his cheek.

"Even though we narrowly escaped spending our idyll with Wesley Templeton?"

"Revolting thought. I've never been so glad to see anyone leave."

"What was his ex-wife like?"

What had she been like? I tried to visualize her in my mind, as she'd been when we were at school together, and afterwards, during her divorce. It was hard for me to think about her without feeling guilty. I hadn't been a very good friend to Sara. I'd tried to be supportive, but she was so needy, I just couldn't handle it. I was a recent widow with an infant to take care of, caught up in my own pain. I didn't have the energy to hold her hand or listen *ad infinitum* to all the gory details.

"Sara was everyone's mother substitute," I said. "If you'd just broken up with your boyfriend, hated your dorm, or were flunking organic chemistry, you'd go cry on Sara's shoulder. There was a warmth and kindness about her that made people want to tell her their troubles. She couldn't have picked a profession which suited her better than clinical psychology."

I conjured her up in my head, a petite dark-haired girl with a heart-shaped face and masses of curly brown hair. She probably had more friends, and was the container for more secrets, than anyone in our class. Yet, paradoxically, she was also one of the most reserved people I knew. Even as a college student, Sara functioned like a therapist. That is to say, she was empathetic and non-judgmental but shared few of her own feelings.

I knew remarkably little about her. She told me she had no family. When she was seven, her father, who was in the garment business, died of a heart attack. Her mother succumbed to cancer when Sara was in high school. I assumed her parents must have left her well provided for. Tuition at Vassar wasn't exactly cheap, but Sara never discussed her financial situation.

True to form, she also told me nothing about her relationship with Wesley. She thanked me for the fix-up, said he was very attractive, and that she would probably go out with him again. I was busy enough with medical school and my own burgeoning romance with Ben, so I didn't pay much attention to anyone else's love life. In fact, I don't think I spared a thought for Sara for a good six months. That was when she told me they were getting married.

"I'm thrilled for you," I said. "I want you to know this is my first successful fix-up ever."

"It's going to be wonderful," Sara said. "Wesley and I have so many plans for working together. We've been talking about joining the Peace Corps after we graduate. I'd like us to use our skills where they're really needed. Or maybe we'll spend a few years on an Indian reservation; someplace where people ordinarily don't have access to good medical or psychiatric care."

Interesting. Wesley hadn't struck me as the Peace Corps type but maybe I'd misjudged him. After all, I'd only met him once. Or maybe Sara's idealism had been contagious. I tried to visualize Wesley in a tent, in the middle of a jungle, passing out malaria pills. The casting didn't fit.

"Has Wesley decided yet about the kind of residency he wants to do?"

"Oh, yes," Sara said. "He's going into surgery. He has wonderful hands."

"Really?" I raised my eyebrows and Sara blushed. "That's a pretty rough training program."

"We know. But I'll have finished my degree by then, and I can work to help support us until he finishes."

"What about his parents. Will they help financially?"

Sara shook her head. "They own a Mom and Pop grocery store in Queens. Wesley went to Yale and Harvard on full scholarships."

I was surprised. "With a name like Templeton, I'd always assumed his dad was a CEO somewhere."

Sara laughed. "Templeton's one of those Ellis Island names. Wesley refuses to tell me what it was before they changed it, but it began with a T and ended with -ski."

"Oh, I see." I said.

Sara and Wesley were married at the Boston Ritz-Carlton by a judge rented for the occasion. The wedding was held in front of the fireplace, in the parlor of the small suite they'd reserved for the night. There were about a dozen guests, mostly classmates. Luncheon with lots of champagne followed the brief ceremony.

"Where are you and Sara going to live when you get back?" I asked Wesley. "Married student housing?"

Wesley laughed. "We just found an incredible apartment. It's the parlor floor of a converted brownstone. It's even got a garden."

"It's a little expensive," Sara said. "But we fell in love with it. I can't wait to fix it up when we get back. As soon as it's ready, I want you and Ben to come over."

I admitted to a tinge of envy. My dorm room at the med school was feeling a little cramped, and I'd have loved to move into Ben's place, even though it would have meant a morning commute across the river. Unfortunately, we'd decided not to live together until we got married the following year. It wouldn't have been worth the arguments it would have provoked on my conservative parental home front. My parents had married very young, but had been in their forties when I was born. They were about a generation behind when it came to sexual mores. I was sure they had completely missed out on the free love of the sixties and seventies.

"We'd love to see it," I told Sara. "Give us a call when you get back from Europe."

I could tell Sara wasn't thinking much about Europe. She seemed to be eyeing the clock, to figure out when she and her new *husband could politely retreat to the bedroom. I said my farewells and made a graceful exit.*

There was a blue sky when we landed at LAX the following afternoon. I decided it was a good omen for the rest of my life. We located Daniel's car in parking lot C and headed north to Brentwood.

"You realize, I'm going to have withdrawal symptoms, not seeing you every day," Daniel said.

"I suspect that when you get back to the office, there'll be so much work on your desk, you won't have time to think about me."

"I am on first call next week," he agreed.

That meant Daniel and his partner would be called for the next murder that occurred. When one happened, they usually worked thirty-six to forty-eight hours straight gathering evidence, always best when it was fresh, and interviewing witnesses. I was just glad that homicide detectives weren't out there on the front lines. By the time they were called in, the danger was usually over.

"Well, if things are quiet, you're always welcome for dinner," I said. "Just let me know, so I can tell Emilia."

"Promise me she won't make anything southern fried." Daniel patted his midsection.

We'd probably both put on five pounds.

"Grilled fish and steamed vegetables," I promised.

I knew he was waiting for me to tell him he could sleep over now, and I didn't know what to say. I still hadn't figured out how I'd explain it to Zoe.

"If it's a quiet weekend, how about I take you and Zoe

out on Saturday? I've got some VIP passes to Universal Studios."

"Zoe would love that," I said. I wasn't so sure about me. I wasn't a great fan of standing in line at theme parks. I was the kind of mother who only took her kid to Disneyland on Super Bowl Sunday. Besides, Daniel wasn't the only one who was going to be on call this week.

Daniel pulled up in front of my townhouse and unloaded my suitcase. Zoe must have been watching from the window because the door opened before I got there.

"Mommy, did you have a good time?" Zoe ran out and held her arms up for a hug.

I lifted her and snuggled her warm little body.

"I missed you," I said. "Did you and Emilia have fun?"

"We got Mittens a baby brother," she said.

"You what?"

Mittens was our gray and white tabby cat. She'd originally belonged to Beth, and was the only eyewitness to her violent end. I'd coaxed her out from under her building with fresh tuna fish and had reluctantly brought her home. Zoe had been campaigning for a pet, and Beth would never have forgiven me if Mittens had been reduced to the ranks of the homeless.

"Look, Mommy."

An orange ball of fluff came bounding out of the house and began to sharpen its tiny claws on my nylons. I was going to have to have a serious talk with Emilia.

Daniel was grinning ear-to-ear, obviously enjoying every minute of my welcome home. He brought my suitcase into the front hall and headed back to his car.

"I'll leave you to unpack," he said. Then he kissed Zoe. "Bye Princess. See you soon."

"Mommy," Zoe said as he drove away. "Why does Daniel always go back to his house? Why can't he stay here?"

CHAPTER SEVEN

D ANIEL'S HOUSE WAS ON THE CORNER OF ONE OF the charming walking streets in Venice; a one story, two-bedroom beach cottage, with a white picket fence, and pots of geraniums on the front porch. Annie had enjoyed gardening, and the curb appeal of the house had deteriorated somewhat since the divorce. The lawn was looking a bit brown. He'd better remember to water it more often in the hot weather.

He drove around to the back alley, parked in his garage, and brought his suitcase in through the back door. The kitchen smelled musty and he opened the window. At least he'd done the dishes before he left last week. He rolled the case through his living room, with its brown leather sofa and Navajo rugs, and into the bedroom. One of the sad things he'd noticed about living alone is that when he came home, his house was exactly the way he left it. In this case, with an unmade bed and a load of laundry.

He drew the laundry bin closer, unpacked his suitcase into it, and dragged it to the laundry room where he unloaded it into the washer. He wasn't really in the mood for doing laundry and errands, but tomorrow was a work day and he might be too exhausted to deal with housekeeping then. He checked the refrigerator and made a list. He was pretty much out of everything except frozen pizza.

Daniel returned to his car, took a quick run to Whole Foods, and stocked up on coffee, eggs, cheese, fresh fruit and vegetables. By the time he got back, his laundry was ready for the dryer. Then, he tackled his mail. As he made a pile of the bills and threw out the ads and catalogues, he found himself feeling lonely and irritable.

It was absurd. He'd only been without Hannah for a couple of hours, and already he missed her. He wanted her in his bed, wanted to wrap himself around her warm, voluptuous body, and to fall asleep listening to her breathing. He understood why she was reluctant to let him spend the night. She wasn't the first woman with a child that he'd dated, but she was the only one he'd ever wanted to be with all the time. He knew he was falling in love with her, and the worst thing he could do was to pressure her, but that didn't keep him from feeling frustrated.

It probably wouldn't hurt to call her, as long as he didn't come across as needy. "Hi there, unpacked yet?"

"Not quite," she said.

"I just called to say goodnight. I miss you."

"Me too," Hannah said. "You and that vacation were exactly what I needed, in that order."

"I'm glad to hear it. Tomorrow could be a brutal day at work. If I don't get a chance to call you, it's not because I'm not thinking about you."

"Same here," Hannah said. "If I'm not available, it's probably because I'm buried in paperwork and they can't dig me out."

"Let's try for the weekend," he said.

"Absolutely."

He hung up, feeling a little better.

CHAPTER EIGHT

THE WEEK OF VACATION HIT ME LIKE A JOLT OF amphetamines. I spent the first day back at work creating a state of virgin purity on my desk top. I signed all my charts in medical records, and returned a week's worth of phone messages. By Tuesday, I was ready to resume seeing patients.

My first patient was Lily Wexler, a thirty-year-old I'd been seeing since my earliest days in practice. Lily was a walking medical miracle who put a smile on my face whenever she entered the office. Her frail, almost childlike, appearance belied her age. It was hard to believe she was more than sixteen. Lily had Gaucher's disease, a recessive genetic disorder in which she lacked a crucial enzyme necessary to break down glycogen, otherwise known as starch, into pieces the body could actually use. As a result, the glycogen accumulated in her liver and spleen. The spleen had been removed a long time ago. The liver grew until it reached her pelvis and distended her abdomen to huge proportions. Her lungs, also a victim of too much extra starch, had lost the ability to expand properly.

When I last saw Lily a year ago, she was barely able to breathe and went everywhere with an oxygen tank. Her lips were blue, her weight barely eighty pounds. I knew she was dying, and there was nothing anyone could do to prevent it. Then, one of those biotech companies in the Silicon Valley genetically-engineered the enzyme Lily needed. Medicare, naturally, refused to pay for it, but the internist who was caring for her obtained private funding so Lily could have it.

She was in for a routine pap smear. She had a normal sized liver, no oxygen tank, had gained thirty pounds, and looked like a million dollars. She even had her very first job. I was thrilled.

I grinned at her as I walked into the exam room.

"You look wonderful," I told her.

I completed her exam, feeling energized and cheerful, and moved on to my next patient.

The next patient was new to my practice, a young girl who'd scheduled herself for a therapeutic abortion the following day. I always see my patients the day before to explain the procedure and draw a preoperative blood type. Shannon had come in with her boyfriend, who was clearly uninterested in becoming a father. She, however, was upset, tearful, and to my mind, too ambivalent to proceed on the following day.

"What do you think I should do?" she asked me in tears, after presenting me with her pros and cons, in great detail.

"I think, perhaps, you should take a little more time and see a therapist who might be able to help you come to a decision," I said. "No one ever goes through this experience without some mixed feelings. I'd like you to be comfortable with whatever decision you make. You still have a few weeks and I'll be happy to help you, whatever you decide."

I had done abortions in my office from day one of my

practice. I was militantly pro-choice. My job was to help my patients make the decisions that worked for them, and to make sure they were implemented in a way that was healthy and safe. When they were having trouble making up their minds, I sent them for skilled, non-judgmental counseling.

I referred her to Dr. Andrea Marcus, my psychiatric consult. Not only was Andrea a great therapist, she was my best friend.

I'd met Andrea Marcus at one of the truly lowest points of my life. Zoe was six months old, which meant she was sleeping through the night. For most mothers, this would have been cause for celebration, but I had relied on my total exhaustion to mask my grief. Everyone I knew thought I'd recovered remarkably from Ben's death. After all, I'd sold my house in Pasadena, bought a condo in Brentwood, hired the perfect live-in housekeeper, given birth, and hadn't missed a beat at the office. What no one seemed to be smart enough to figure out, was that just because you were too tired to think about something, didn't mean you'd actually dealt with it.

The moment my fatigue lifted, depression attacked me like a crowd of killer bees. I couldn't go to bed at night, without bursting into tears, because I had no one to cuddle. I fondled Ben's coffee cup at breakfast. I spent hours studying every picture we'd ever been organized enough to put in an album, and I stopped being able to concentrate on anything else.

The worst part of it was that there was no one I could talk to. I hadn't cultivated any intimate friendships during the years of my marriage. I hadn't needed to. Ben had been husband, lover, playmate and best friend. If I needed a confidante, all I had to do was to get his attention over dinner. We'd had social friends, of course. There had been lots of people to party with, but they were couple friends. There was no one with whom I could be vulnerable.

Actually, that wasn't quite true. There was Ben's sister, Beth, whom I loved and trusted as if she were my own. But, Beth had enough of her own problems, and I didn't want to exacerbate her grief over Ben by burdening her with mine. Somewhere in the middle of all that, one of the female physicians in my department invited me to a fundraiser for Emily's List. I was totally uninterested in socializing, but she wouldn't take no for an answer.

Andrea had engaged me in conversation over a bowl of guacamole. Without doubt, she was one of the most beautiful women I'd ever seen. Actress or model, I had concluded, either that, or a wealthy Beverly Hills wife. I checked her left hand for rings.

To my embarrassment, she turned out to be a psychiatrist in private practice. I'd berated myself for thinking like a male chauvinist and wondered if Andrea's sensational looks had been a handicap during medical school.

I can't remember what we talked about that night, only that we talked non-stop until the end of the reception, and that she invited me to have brunch with her the following Sunday. I accepted, recognizing that we'd connected with a special sense of chemistry that told me we could be genuine friends.

I wish I could say that the friendship had come easily but it hadn't. Andrea and I were both very private people, slow to trust, and hesitant to reveal ourselves. We feinted with one another like a dating couple, each reluctant to be the first to expose anything real. It took almost six months until the night I found myself crying into my coffee and telling her all about Ben. I've never regretted it.

CHAPTER NINE

Periodically, during the course of the day, I found myself thinking about Sara. Should I tell her I'd seen Wesley? Should I call and find out how she was doing? I couldn't decide. It had been at least four years since I'd spoken to her. I didn't even know if she still lived in Beverly Hills. They'd had a house there, but I was pretty sure it had gotten sold at the time of the divorce.

Finally, I went online and checked the White Pages. There was no listing in Beverly Hills for a Sara Hellman or a Sara Templeton. The Los Angeles phone book also drew a blank and I had no idea where else to look. She could have moved anywhere, and knowing Sara, her phone number was probably unlisted. Of course, Daniel had access to the DMV files. If I really wanted to find her, all I had to do was to ask him. I reached for the phone and then put it down. I just wasn't ready to deal with it. Sara's unhappiness had been contagious and I'd just come out of a year of misery. This was the first time in ages I'd felt truly happy and I didn't want anything to spoil it.

It was such a shame. I remembered how happy they'd seemed those first few years in Cambridge. They'd invited Ben and me over when the fall semester started. We arrived, bearing a bottle of Soave Bola and a philodendron as a housewarming gift. We'd been expecting the usual student apartment: moldy wallpaper from the 1930's, brick and board bookcases, big floor pillows and lots of houseplants. When they opened the door, I thought we'd gone to the wrong house.

The parlor was spectacular. Peg and groove floors had been stained very dark and gleamed from polish. The walls were painted forest green with a white trim highlighting the elaborate molding. The fireplace was white marble.

The floor was covered with an expensive-looking oriental rug. A sofa and two wing chairs, in green and pink chintz, flanked the fireplace. At the other end of the room, stood a mahogany breakfront displaying new china, and a large dining table with eight chairs. I couldn't tell the difference between real antiques and antique reproductions, but it all looked very expensive. The accessories were Oriental, a large Chinese screen, beautifully framed Japanese prints, and heavy Chinese vases.

"This place come furnished or what?" Ben asked.

Sara giggled. "Do you like it? I decorated myself. Wesley wanted us to live like grown-ups."

"I've always thought antiques were a good investment," Wesley said. "If we get bored with them, and want to redecorate later on, we can always sell them at a profit."

"Let me get us a snack before we go out to dinner," Sara said.

Sara never seemed to cook and I wondered if we'd ever get to sit down to dinner at that exquisitely polished antique dining table.

"I was running late this afternoon," she said. "I haven't even had time to unpack the groceries."

I accompanied her into her tiny, immaculate kitchen and waited while she transferred her purchases into the pantry. The pantry was arranged with military precision, in what I swear looked like alphabetical order. Sara removed each can from the bag, washed it off with a moist sponge, and put it away. Then she set out a tray with wine glasses, cold white wine, crackers, and Brie.

"I made us dinner reservations at a new Greek place in Boston," Wesley said. "I'll drive."

"He just wants to show off his new car," Sara said, with a look that implied that men were such children.

"Well, I bought the car as an investment," Wesley said. "Everyone knows that Mercedes makes the best cars in the world. They last forever and they hold their value for resale."

"Of course," Ben said. Ben was driving a 1989 Valiant, which was on its last legs, and from which he refused to be parted. "Did you have a windfall at the track or something?"

Wesley put an arm around Sara, and drew her to him. "Not at all, I just married an heiress."

Sara smiled at him fondly. "He probably married me for my money."

"Not so. I married you for your body."

Sara blushed.

"Well," I said. "Looks like you're going to have to put a lot of stuff in storage when you join the Peace Corps."

I thought about Sara for another twenty-four hours, before changing my mind and asking Daniel to try to trace her, berating myself for behaving like a self-centered brat. Sara had been a good friend to me for years. I'd withdrawn out of self-preservation, unable to cope with her neediness when I was in mourning, but enough was enough. By my own admission, I was feeling truly happy and functional for the first time since Ben died. I could certainly manage to extend myself far enough to make one phone call.

It took Daniel about half an hour to find Sara. She was living in Santa Monica, probably no more than a few minutes from my house in Brentwood. The address suggested an apartment or condominium. Before I could change my mind, I picked up the receiver, then I paused. A conversation with Sara couldn't possibly take place during the five minutes I had between patients in the office. I'd have to find a free hour, one of these evenings.

I hadn't seen Daniel all week, so I figured he'd been up to his armpits in work, just as I had.

When he called my office Friday morning, I assumed it was social.

"Hi," I said. "Are you calling to invite yourself to dinner?"

"I wish," he said. "I'm calling to give you some bad news before you hear it on television. There's been a murder at West Beverly Hospital. Someone you know."

"Someone I know?"

"I'm afraid so," Daniel said. "The victim's been identified as Dr. Wesley Templeton."

CHAPTER TEN

"You're not serious," I said.

"I'm afraid I am," Daniel said. "I'm on my way over to West Beverly, as we speak."

My stomach twisted itself into a knot. This was the second time that someone I knew had been a murder victim. Of course, I had adored Beth, and Wesley wasn't exactly on my A-list, but I wouldn't wish murder on my worst enemy.

"Poor Sara," I said.

"Why, poor Sara?"

"She was living on the alimony checks. Wesley managed to spend all the money she inherited from her parents on his fancy cars and antiques. The last I saw, she wasn't functional enough to support herself. I told you, it was a vicious divorce. I wonder if he left life insurance."

"If he did, that might be one motive for murder," Daniel said. "You realize, I'm going to have to talk to Sara?"

"I know, but Sara can't possibly be a serious suspect. Wesley was a despicable man. You'll probably find a whole line-up of people with motives to kill him. How did he die?"

"I don't know yet. I think we'll need the autopsy report to find out. Do you happen to know anything about West Beverly?" Daniel asked.

"Of course," I said. "I have staff privileges there. I use it occasionally, when I can't get a surgical case on at Memorial. I don't like it much."

"Why not?"

"It's exclusive, private and very expensive. It's the sort of place the rich and famous go when they need to have their hemorrhoids removed in total privacy with maximum pampering. The staff has lots of celebrity docs who admit their poor patients to Los Angeles Memorial. Memorial is friendlier, has better medical care and better surgical instruments. I'm not surprised that Wesley was operating at West Beverly. He must have had a very wealthy clientele."

"Thanks. It's always useful to get a sense of a place before you barge in and start asking questions. I'll call you later, and let you know what I can, when I finish up the crime scene work."

Daniel maintained strict confidentiality when it came to his ongoing cases, just as I protected the privacy of my patients. However, if my old friend Sara was on the list of suspects, I intended to pump him for as much information as I could extract, and do anything I could, to help him find the real killer.

The Templetons had remained in Boston, after Ben and I moved to Los Angeles and settled into our Craftsman bungalow in Pasadena. Wesley had a general surgery residency at Mass. General and Sara got a job as a school psychologist, at an inner-city school with a Head Start program. We exchanged cards

every Christmas, but that was the extent of our contact. Friendships don't flower three thousand miles apart, so I was surprised one day to get a call from Sara.

"How nice to hear from you," I said. "Where are you?"

"You'll never guess," she said. "We've just moved to Pasadena. Wesley decided to switch to plastic surgery and he's finishing his residency at USC."

She gave me an address on Del Mar Boulevard and we arranged for the four of us to go out for dinner.

Their apartment was in a posh new building I'd noticed going up the year before. It was spacious, modern and crammed with even more antiques than the old one had been, not to mention a top-of-the-line television with a giant screen. Not for the first time, I wondered if the two of them were blowing Sara's inheritance. Residents weren't that well paid.

Sara had a new job at a County mental health clinic in Alhambra, and her dinner table conversation was filled with complaints about how inadequate the resources were for poor people.

"I saw a new client today with a severe postpartum psychosis," she said. "Her husband brought her in, because he was terrified she was going to kill their baby. If she had money, she'd be hospitalized, medicated, and properly treated. As it is, all I can do is to offer outpatient therapy once a week, and it's not enough."

"Sara is continually disappointed that she can't personally solve all the world's problems," Wesley said.

I thought it was one of her nicer qualities. So did Ben. I could see from the glance Ben gave me that he didn't appreciate Wesley's sarcasm.

Wesley's conversation was full of the surgical pyrotechnics he was performing as part of the university's craniofacial team, reconstructing a normal appearance for children born with severe facial abnormalities.

During those years, I counted the Templetons among our closest friends. We spent lots of time together: theatre, movies, barbecues in our tiny back yard, dinners at trendy new restaurants usually discovered by Wesley. Sara was always warm and welcoming, Wesley was always witty and charming. Yet, when I look back, it seems to me that there was no real intimacy.

Sara and Wesley were one of those married couples who were sufficient unto themselves. They seemed completely absorbed in one another, and in absolutely no need of any outside confidante. I'd never heard Sara voice the slightest disapproval of anything Wesley said, did or wanted, and it would never have occurred to me to ask her if he was good in bed or if he did the dishes. There was a wall around their perfect marriage, and though they entertained frequently at its periphery, they never let anyone in.

Ben and I had speculated on what Wesley and Sara would do when Wesley finished his residency. Ben, being more idealistic than I, thought they'd take a year or two off, and live out Sara's fantasy of the Peace Corps. I put my money on private practice and won, hands down.

"I just got a fabulous offer to go in with Mort Levine in Beverly Hills," Wesley said one night, during his last residency year.

"Who's he?" I asked.

"You know, he's married to Ashley Mortimer, the actress. Rumor has it, he's operated on every part of her anatomy. He's got a big celebrity practice with an office on Lasky Drive," Wesley said.

"I thought that was where all the shrinks practiced," Ben said.

Sara laughed. "Wesley said I should go into private practice and rent an office next door."

"Are you going to?" I asked.

"I don't think so, but I am going to have to look for a new job.

I don't want to commute from Beverly Hills to Alhambra every day, and Wesley wants us to live close to his office."

"No Peace Corps?" I asked.

Sara looked rueful. "I guess not. I suppose it was just a childish fantasy."

The Templetons left Pasadena and rented an apartment on Doheny Drive in Beverly Hills. For a while, we kept in touch, until I realized that all the phone calls and all the invitations were coming from me.

"It's their turn," I told Ben. "I feel like we do all the work of maintaining this friendship. If they care about us, then let them make the next call."

They never did call.

But, we ran into them one morning when we'd taken an excursion from Pasadena to Beverly Hills, to have brunch at Nate and Al's.

"So nice to see you," Wesley had said, as if they'd seen us just the other day.

Sara had hugged me with genuine warmth.

They'd joined us for breakfast, and then insisted we come back to their place to view their latest project. We'd spent the next two hours making polite noises over the architectural plans for their dream house, a little five-bedroom place they were building, on a lot they'd bought just off Benedict Canyon. We only got to see the finished product once, before they disappeared from our lives again.

D ANIEL TURNED OFF HIS CELL PHONE AND PULLED into the patient parking lot at West Beverly Hospital, feeling disconcerted over his conversation with Hannah. The last thing he wanted to do was to involve her in this investigation. Even though she hadn't particularly liked Wesley, he was still a murder victim she knew, and he remembered how stressed she had been during the search for Beth's killer. He'd be walking a fine line between satisfying her curiosity and keeping her at arm's length.

He walked around to the front entrance, where a police barricade was keeping the press at bay. Several patrol cars and the crime team vans were parked in the driveway.

He approached one of the patrolmen and presented his ID.

"They're in the operating suite in the basement, Detective. Just take the elevator down. You won't have any trouble finding them."

The elevator deposited him in a stark white corridor. A bright blue arrow indicated that the operating suite was to the left. A pair of automatic doors proclaimed "Authorized Personnel Only, Surgical Attire Required." Just before he reached the doors, the corridor branched to the right, where the police activity was centered on the entrance to the men's locker room.

He spotted Dr. William Pincus, one of the Coroner's forensic specialists.

Bill saw Daniel and waved, a broad smile splitting his pudgy lined face. "Nice to see you, Dan."

Bill was approaching retirement, and had probably seen more dead bodies than anyone else Daniel knew. He was known for his gruff manner and complete intolerance for stupidity. Daniel loved having him on his cases because he rarely missed a detail.

"I wish it was a pleasanter occasion," Daniel said. "How'd he die?"

"Interesting question. Come have a look. They haven't moved him yet."

Daniel followed Bill into the locker room.

The police photographer was getting the body from every angle he could manage.

Wesley had been in front of his locker, bare-chested and wearing surgical scrub pants. It looked as though he'd bent down to get something and someone had shoved his head inside. He was on his knees, arms dangling, head resting on the locker floor. Rigor mortis had set in, and the blood had pooled in the lower portion of his body, leaving his face a hideous, swollen blue.

Daniel could only imagine how Hannah would react to the sight.

"I don't see any knife or bullet wounds. What makes you so sure this is a homicide, not a heart attack?" Daniel asked.

"I won't be a hundred percent certain, until I run the toxicology," Bill said. "But look at this."

Bill put on a pair of latex gloves and exposed Wesley's neck. A large blue contusion, with what appeared to be a needle mark in its center, marred the area of the right carotid artery.

"Not a flu shot, I take it," Daniel said.

"I think not," Bill said. "Looks like someone snuck up behind him, shoved his head in the locker and gave him an injection."

"Well, there's certainly enough lethal stuff around an operating room. When did it happen?"

"Somewhere between midnight and one," Bill said. "Body's still stiff as a board, but the lividity doesn't blanch."

He demonstrated by pressing a finger to the blue chest. Up to eight hours after death, finger pressure creates a white mark. After eight hours, the skin stays blue.

"We know he was alive at ten past midnight, because he was seen in the recovery room." Bill said, motioning Daniel back into the hallway. "I don't think you need me anymore. I'm going to get back to work and wait for your friend to arrive downtown."

Daniel nodded. "Let me know as soon as you've finished the autopsy."

The office of the Operating Room Charge Nurse had been converted into a temporary command post. A pot of coffee was sitting on a side table, and he poured some into a Styrofoam cup, motioning to the officer who had been first on the scene to come in.

"What do we know so far?" Daniel asked.

"Not much," the officer said. "Most of the staff who were here last night are home sleeping this morning. I'm having them all brought in for questioning. Apparently, there was an automobile accident. A woman named Veronica Hayden, a young actress, had severe facial lacerations from the broken windshield. They brought her to the emergency room and Dr. Templeton was called in, at her request, to repair her face. I wouldn't be surprised if he created the face in the first place."

"I didn't know this hospital even had an emergency room," Daniel said. Hannah had made it sound more like a fancy nursing home.

"It's not exactly part of the County Trauma Network," the officer said. "They maintain it mostly for the convenience of their staff. I understand it's a plum moonlighting job for L.A. County residents, because they get to sleep most nights. Anyway, they paged Templeton and he came in around nine-thirty p.m. and operated. Finished a little before midnight, according to the anesthesia record."

"How many people were in the operating suite last night?" Daniel asked.

"Not many. This was the only surgical case. They called in a scrub tech, a circulating nurse, and an anesthesiologist. They have one nurse who works the night shift, carries the emergency surgery beeper, and who doubles in the recovery room, if it's a slow night. She was the last person to see him, except for his killer."

"What's the access like to the operating suite and the hospital at night?" Daniel asked. "Could an outside person have gotten in unobserved?"

"If they knew where they were going and were lucky. The front entrance is unlocked all night. There's a security guard at the front desk, but he makes rounds, so I suppose someone could slip in when the desk was empty. But the killer wouldn't have had to sneak in at midnight. He could have come in earlier, during visiting hours, and not left. Or it could be any hospital employee on the upper floors. In surgical scrubs, or a nursing uniform, anyone could go anywhere in a hospital and be invisible."

"You're absolutely right," said Daniel. "He could even have been killed by a patient, although that seems a little farfetched. It seems to me, we need to start with the staff who saw him last night, and with his present and ex-wives. Maybe we can establish a motive."

"Has anyone told either of them yet?"

Daniel nodded. "I called on my way over, and sent a policewoman to break the news to his wife, but no one's told the ex. I thought I'd do that myself."

CHAPTER TWELVE

D ANIEL CHECKED THE TEMPLETONS’ ADDRESS AND headed for his squad car. It was on North Canon Drive in the Beverly Hills Flats, from which he deduced that Wesley’s plastic surgery practice had been thriving. You couldn’t touch the real estate on that street for less than five million.

Wesley Templeton’s home was a massive mansion, pretending to be a French chateau. Tall hedges bordered the property, and the circular driveway was surrounded by gardens that were no less formal, if slightly smaller, than those at Versailles. A police car was parked at the front door.

Daniel parked behind it and the driver, a stocky woman, with short blonde hair, wearing a police uniform, stepped out to meet him. Sergeant Brenda Jordan had worked with Daniel on a number of cases and was particularly skilled at breaking bad news. He always liked to partner with her. She was smart, tough and very professional.

“I’m glad you’re here, sir.”

“Did you tell her?” he asked.

Brenda nodded. “She got pretty hysterical for a while.

Her housekeeper took her upstairs for a Valium. She's expecting you, but I don't know if you'll get much useful information. God, I hate this part of the job."

"I know," Daniel said. "Everyone does. You'll need to come in with me and record the interview."

He rang the doorbell.

They were let in by the housekeeper and shown into the living room.

"I'll get Mrs. Templeton," the housekeeper said. "She'll be a few minutes."

He looked around with interest. The house looked architecturally authentic, as if it had been built in the 20s or 30s, and tastefully brought into the twenty-first century. It was done all in pastels, mostly pale blue, with French antique furniture, light woods and expensive-looking impressionist paintings. Nose jobs appeared to be a lucrative business.

"I'm sorry to keep you waiting." Erica Templeton walked down the curved staircase, into the front hall, and joined them in the living room.

The combination of tears and no make-up made her horse-face look even more unattractive than he'd remembered. He was disposed to dislike her on principle. After all, she was the other woman in Hannah's roommate's divorce, but he couldn't help feeling sorry for her. He knew what those initial few moments of shock, pain and disbelief could feel like.

"I'm sorry to intrude on you, Mrs. Templeton," Daniel said. "But an unexplained death of this kind is a police matter and I need to ask you a few questions. My name is Daniel Ross. I'm a detective with the LAPD. You've already met my colleague, Sergeant Jordan."

Erica acknowledged their presence, as if she'd never seen him before. He wondered if she was just in too much shock to make the connection to Marianne's Key, or if she'd genuinely forgotten having met him. It was just as well.

"I don't understand," Erica said. "The sergeant said Wesley was found dead in the locker room at West Beverly. How did he die?"

"We aren't certain yet, ma'am. We'll need the autopsy report to determine the exact cause of death, but it looks as though he may have been murdered."

Erica's eyes widened. "I can't believe that."

"May I have your permission to record this interview, Mrs. Templeton? It helps us keep all the little details straight."

She nodded. "Go ahead. What do you want to ask me?"

"When was the last time you saw your husband?" Daniel said.

"About seven-thirty. We were just sitting down to dinner when his exchange called. Wesley told me he had to leave because of some surgical emergency. He told me not to wait up, that he'd probably be late."

"Did he get emergency calls often?"

Erica shook her head. "Fortunately not. Plastic surgery tends not to generate too many emergencies."

"Weren't you concerned, when you realized he hadn't come home last night?" Daniel asked.

"I didn't realize. I don't sleep very well, Detective Ross. I usually need earplugs, a mask, and a sleeping pill to get to sleep. And if I'm disturbed in the middle of the night, I'm awake for the duration. Wesley made it a point not to disturb me with a late arrival. If he came home after I went to bed, he'd sleep in one of the guest rooms."

"Did that happen often?" Daniel asked.

"Usually once or twice a week. My husband was very

active in his profession. He was always going to meetings of hospital committees and medical societies."

"Did your husband have any medical problems, a bad heart for example?" Daniel asked.

"Wesley was completely healthy," Erica said. "He was fanatic about keeping in shape. He used to work out at the gym at least four times a week, and when he wasn't at the gym, he jogged or swam. He had the body of a twenty-year-old." Her mouth trembled.

"How long were you married, Mrs. Templeton?" Daniel asked.

"We just celebrated our third anniversary, two weeks ago." Her eyes filled with tears.

"How did you meet?"

"I used to work for Wesley. I did his insurance billing and bookkeeping."

"That was when he was still married to his first wife?" Daniel asked.

She nodded. "Wesley was so unhappy. His wife was a chronic depressive. He took care of her, devotedly, for years. But finally, he couldn't stand living with someone who was mentally ill anymore, so they were divorced."

"An unpleasant divorce?" he asked.

The tremulous mouth hardened. "She made his life, and mine, a living hell. She's still doing it. She takes him back to court every chance she gets."

"Mrs. Templeton, did your husband have any enemies? Can you think of anyone who disliked him enough to want him dead?"

"You're implying he was murdered," she said. "I still find that impossible to believe."

"As I said, the evidence isn't complete yet, but if it does

turn out to be murder, and there are reasons to think it is, I'd value your help right now."

"You could start with that bitch, his ex-wife," she said. "I can't think of anyone who'll be happier to hear that he died."

"Wasn't he supporting her with alimony?" Daniel asked. "Would she want to kill the source of her financial support?" His transient sympathy for Erica had evaporated.

"That assumes her thought processes are rational," Erica said. "The woman's crazy, and she hated Wesley with a passion."

"Does she stand to inherit any life insurance because of his death?" Daniel asked.

Erica shrugged. "You'd have to ask Wesley's lawyer. I wasn't involved in their financial settlement."

"Anyone else you can think of, Mrs. Templeton? Someone who worked at the hospital, a business or professional associate with a grudge?"

Erica shook her head. "Wesley was in partnership with another plastic surgeon. There was some talk recently about dissolving the partnership. Wesley didn't feel he was getting his fair share of the profits, but I can't imagine Dr. Levine as a murderer."

"Mrs. Templeton, are you familiar with the layout of the operating suite at West Beverly? Did you ever go there, to pick up your husband, for example?" Daniel asked.

"Occasionally, I'd meet him in the doctor's lounge on the first floor," she said.

Daniel nodded. "Just one more question, ma'am. How did you spend the rest of the evening after Dr. Templeton left?"

"Are you asking me for an alibi, detective?" she said.

"Just curious."

"I finished my dinner, went to my room and read until ten-thirty. Then I went to sleep. You can ask Gladys, the live-in, if you need confirmation." Her lips clamped tightly together. "Is that all, detective?"

"For now, Mrs. Templeton. Please accept my condolences on your loss. We'll let you know as soon as the cause of death has been determined. I'm sure you'll want to make arrangements. We should be able to release your husband's body to you in a few days. I'll be in touch."

Daniel rose and signaled the Sergeant to leave.

Erica preceded them out of the living room and headed up the staircase. "Gladys will show you out," she said.

Daniel turned to Brenda. "Go ahead and interview the housekeeper, will you? You know what to ask. When you're done, grab something to eat and meet me at the hospital. We'll be interviewing the staff from last night, as soon they come in."

Brenda nodded and he headed for his car.

As he got in, planning to drive south toward Santa Monica Boulevard, he noticed a dingy blue Honda parked across the street from the Templeton's garage. It was the sort of car favored by plainclothes cops, but he didn't think it was one of theirs. Out of habit, he made a note of the license plate and then headed east instead, back to the hospital.

CHAPTER THIRTEEN

I T'S A GOOD THING THAT TODAY WAS AN OFFICE DAY, and we were packed with patients. If I'd been at home, I would be pacing the floor like a caged lion, waiting for Daniel to call me and tell me what had really happened. As it was, every time I returned to my consult room, I checked my desk to see if any of the pink message slips that had accumulated were from him. I knew better. Daniel wasn't going to call me in the middle of his investigation any more than I would phone him during a surgery. I was going to have to wait patiently until the end of the day, and patience was not one of my major virtues.

During my lunch hour (yogurt at my desk), I thought some more about Sara. I was feeling doubly guilty. Despite my determination to call her, I had procrastinated. It never seemed like the right time to settle in for a protracted, and probably depressing, conversation. I was a lousy friend. The truth was that the Sara who had been my roommate and friend had morphed into a person I barely knew. The only thing I was sure of in my gut was that, as much as she hated Wesley, Sara didn't have the capacity to kill. I tried to remember what I had learned about him, from her, that might help Daniel find the real murderer.

Our friendship with the Templetons never revived itself. We'd received a change of address notice, and an invitation to the housewarming they threw after they moved into their magnum opus, which we attended. We never heard from them afterwards. In any case, about two years later, Ben became ill and I became pregnant. After the death of my husband, and the birth of my daughter, the last thing I was interested in was pursuing dinner parties with old friends who never called.

About two years after Zoe's birth, Sara phoned me at the office.

"Hannah?"

The voice on the other end of the phone was so low, I could barely hear it, let alone recognize it.

"It's Sara. Sara Templeton."

"Sara? You sound awful. Is something wrong?"

"I know I haven't called in a long time, but I just couldn't. Wesley and I are getting a divorce. I threw him out of the house, a few weeks ago."

I was stunned. "I always thought you and Wesley had the perfect marriage. You seemed so bonded to one another, as though there was no one else in the whole world."

"It was a lie," she said. "My whole marriage was a lie and a sham. I was married to him for eighteen years and he deceived me from the very first day. Nothing about him was what it appeared to be. He was leading a complete double life."

She started to cry, great wracking sobs, the sort of cries that admit no comfort, especially over the phone.

"I'm so sorry," I said. "I can't imagine how awful you must feel."

"I was driving his car to the supermarket and I opened the trunk to put my groceries away. I found an old bill from our florist, for Valentine's Day. That's how I found out he was having an affair. I never got any flowers."

"The bastard. Who is she?" I asked.

"His office manager. He was always coming home late because he had to review the accounts with her, and taking her to office lunches. I was so naïve, it never occurred to me he was going to bed with her."

"Sara, lots of marriages have survived affairs. Did you and Wesley consider conjoint therapy?"

"You don't understand. We were married for eighteen years, and the whole time he was telling me he loved me, from the very beginning at Harvard, he had other women. My whole life, everything I thought was real, was a lie."

I'd never heard anyone in so much pain. I didn't know what to do or say to her, or what she expected of me after all this time.

"I can't stay on the phone much longer," I said. "But I'd like to see you, if you want some company."

She started to cry again. "He sabotaged all my friendships, isolated me from everyone I cared about. There's no reason you should even want to be my friend."

This wasn't a conversation I could deal with in the middle of a busy office day. I promised to drop by on my way home from work.

When Sara opened the door, I barely recognized her. When I thought of her, the image I evoked had always been of the college girl of twenty years ago—delicate, petite, vibrant. She had become a faded old woman. More than faded, she looked as if she'd been in a concentration camp. Her body was wasted, her face gaunt. Skin *sagged from her chin and throat. Her magnificent head of thick curly hair was completely gray, and hung uncombed around her face. She was wearing a sleeveless nightgown that was wrinkled and stained.*

"I'm so glad you're here." Sara threw herself into my arms and held onto me crying.

The scent of cigarette smoke clung to her hair. I patted her shoulder awkwardly, torn between my empathy and my discomfort, and eased her back into the house.

"I thought you weren't home," I said. "It took you so long to answer the door."

"I heard the doorbell," she said. "I tried to mobilize myself to get up and answer it, but I couldn't."

I looked around the living room. It was beautifully proportioned and decorated with antiques I recognized, and many I'd never seen before. Every surface I could see was covered with piles of paper—the floors, the stairs, the tables and chairs, the sofa.

She moved a pile and motioned me to sit down.

"What is all this stuff?" I asked. I'd never seen the slightest hint of clutter or disorder in any of Sara's homes. Her passion for neatness had been obsessive.

"Every paper in our file cabinet. I've got to organize them and read them all. The evidence is there, if I can just trace it—every bit of financial deception, every affair. I know it's all there. There isn't enough time. I've got to read it, before he breaks in here and steals it. I know he's tapping my phone and following me. I went to the store last week, and when I came back, some of the piles weren't where I'd left them."

"Slow down," I said.

She was sitting hunched over, wringing her hands, tapping her right foot. I thought she'd jump out of her chair in a second. I'd never seen anyone so literally vibrating in place.

"I'm going to make us both a cup of tea, and then you can tell me all about it, from the beginning." I went into the kitchen, filled

the kettle with water and searched the cupboards for some mugs and tea bags. I brewed two cups of Darjeeling and brought them into the living room.

Sara was smoking a cigarette, a habit she'd had for years and had never been able to give up. I noticed a large pile of butts in the ashtray.

I handed her a cup and retreated to the other end of the living room, as far away from the smoke as I could get. "Tell me about it, Sara."

"I was so happy and in love with him, when we were dating at Harvard. He was romantic and attentive, such a passionate lover. But it all started falling apart after the honeymoon. I thought he shared my values, really wanted to help other people, but he was a greedy acquisitive bastard. He never seemed to have enough things, always had to have the biggest and the best—antique furniture, Mercedes, hi-fi's, workout equipment. You name it, it's probably here somewhere.

"When my parents died, they left me a hundred thousand dollars. That was big money in those days. If I'd invested it, I'd be a wealthy woman now. But, oh no, the Bank of Sara spent all that money keeping Wesley in the lifestyle to which he wanted to become accustomed. Then, he finished his residency and became a hot shot Beverly Hills plastic surgeon and really started going berserk.

"Most young couples buy their first home. Not the Templetons! We had to build one using the most expensive architect in town, and Sara had to quit her job to supervise the construction. How do you like it? I call it my mausoleum." She started to cry again.

"It's a lovely house," I said. I located a box of tissues and braved the cloud of smoke to hand it to her. "I guess you can never know from the outside what someone's marriage is really like.

Ben and I always saw you two as so close to one another, that you didn't need anyone else."

"I heard about Ben," Sara said. "I'm so sorry, Hannah. I wanted to call you but I was too depressed, I couldn't."

"I thought you and Wesley weren't interested in being friends with us anymore. The only times we ever saw you were when I called. You never seemed to reciprocate."

"I know," she said. "I wanted to, but Wesley would never let me. Every time I suggested calling any of our friends and inviting them for dinner, he'd always have an excuse as to why we couldn't, or why he didn't like them anymore. After a while, we stopped seeing everyone. I missed you."

"Did you know Ben and I had a child?"

Sara shook her head. "I'm glad for you. Wesley never wanted to have children. Now, I understand why. They would have interfered with his tootsies."

"Are you sure there were that many?" I asked.

"Oh, I'm sure. He had an affair at Harvard the first year we were married. I found out about it and almost left him, but he begged me not to and promised he'd never do it again. I was stupid enough to believe him."

"I don't think you were stupid," I said, my heart going out to her. "I imagine the signs were all there. You probably just couldn't bear to allow yourself to see them."

"I know you're right," Sara said. "It was so classic. He was always working late or having business dinners. In all the years we were married, we only took one vacation together. Every time I wanted to go away, he had a medical conference he had to attend. He never took me with him. He always said I'd be bored. I'll bet his mistresses weren't bored."

"Is there anything I can do for you?" I asked, not really believing anything I could do would touch the core of her misery.

"Happen to know a vicious divorce lawyer?" she asked.

So, he'd had multiple mistresses, was greedy and acquisitive, and might have had a few shady financial dealings. There were lots of possible motives to share with Daniel, when he got around to calling me. In the meantime, I was going to find out whatever I could, and try to be a better friend to Sara.

CHAPTER FOURTEEN

IT WAS ABOUT TWELVE-THIRTY P.M., WHEN DANIEL returned to West Beverly Hospital. The evening shift was due in to be questioned at two p.m., which gave him some time to interview Wesley's last patient. Although she clearly had a perfect alibi, in recovery from general anesthesia at the time of the murder, he thought that perhaps she might remember who else was in the recovery room with her and when.

Veronica Hayden looked like she'd just come from a casting call for *The Return of the Mummy*. Her head and face were swathed in a hood of white bandages, which covered most of her cheeks, forehead, nose and chin. The eyes peering out from the mask looked very young and vulnerable. They were a deep blue, with long black lashes, the effect somewhat spoiled by the two shiners that surrounded them. She had wide, beautifully shaped lips, with perfect teeth and a tiny black beauty mark at the corner of her mouth. Even with the bandages, you could tell she'd probably been beautiful. He wondered if Wesley had done a good job sewing her up.

"Miss Hayden, I'm police detective Ross. I know you must be in pain right now, but I wonder if I could have just a few minutes of your time."

Veronica forced a smile. "It's okay, I just had a pain pill. Is it about Dr. Templeton?"

"You heard?" Daniel asked.

"It's been the talk of the hospital," she said. "The nurses are saying it might be murder. I just can't believe it. He was such a wonderful man."

"Did you know Dr. Templeton before your accident?" he asked.

She nodded. "I moved to Los Angeles about a year ago, so I could start an acting career. I had a rather large nose, which didn't look good on film, so my agent suggested I see him. Dr. Templeton did a wonderful job for me. When this happened, I asked them to call him."

"How did it happen?" Daniel asked.

She shook her head. "I was driving north on Robertson. I was supposed to meet a friend for dinner at eight, and someone ran a red light and smashed into me. The windshield shattered. That's almost all I remember, until I got to the emergency room and they told me my face was badly cut up, and I was going to need plastic surgery. I was so lucky they managed to reach the doctor."

"Do you remember seeing him at all after your surgery?" Daniel asked.

"He was there just as I was waking up. I was so groggy, I don't think I really looked at him. I just remember his voice saying, "Surgery's over, Veronica. Everything's fine. You're going to be as pretty as ever." Her eyes misted.

"Was anyone else in the recovery room with you?"

"Just the nurse," Veronica said. "An African-American woman."

"Was she in the recovery room the whole time you were?" he asked.

"I guess so," she said. "I dozed off a lot from the pain medication they gave me, but she always seemed to be there whenever I woke up."

"Do you have any idea of what time it was when they took you from recovery to your room?" Daniel asked.

"About two a.m.," she said. "There was a big clock, just opposite my bed."

Daniel nodded and turned off his tape recorder. "Thanks, Miss Hayden. You've been a big help. I hope you have an uneventful recovery."

He left the room and stopped at the nursing station to look at her chart. According to the E.R. sheet, Veronica had arrived by ambulance at 8:35 p.m. They'd started an IV, drawn blood, done a CT scan for head injury, and x-rayed her for broken bones, and had arranged for Wesley to repair her shattered face. Shards of glass had made several very deep cuts and barely missed her right eye. The anesthesiologist's record showed that the patient entered the operating room at 10:07 p.m., and general anesthesia was induced at 10:20 p.m. Surgery started at 10:25 p.m. and ended at 11:50 p.m. The patient was extubated and transferred to the recovery room at 12:00 a.m. The recovery room sheet showed vital signs in the same handwriting, every fifteen minutes, until the patient was sent to her room at 1:55 a.m.

Of course, the chart didn't exonerate the recovery room nurse. She could have faked the data and left the room to murder Wesley, while Veronica was sleeping. She could even have given her medication, to be sure she slept. It would be nice to know for sure whether he really was murdered. Everything always seemed to take too long downtown. He debated calling Bill, but decided against it. The pathologist would call him when he had something.

Daniel was finding it difficult to concentrate. It had been a long time since he'd had a vacation, and the abrupt transition from idyllic beaches and exciting lovemaking to grisly murder was a challenge. Thoughts of Hannah kept intruding, and he forced them to the back of his mind. He needed to focus. He promised himself he would call her, as soon as he had a free minute.

He retreated to his temporary command headquarters. The crime team had finished taking whatever samples there were to take, and the hospital housekeeping crew was busy scrubbing fingerprint powder off the walls and lockers. Brenda arrived, right on time, and the young patrolman Daniel had assigned to the job of collecting witnesses brought in the recovery room nurse, Martha Wells.

Mrs. Wells was middle-aged and black, with a gentle face and frizzy hair streaked with gray.

She sat down calmly opposite them and smiled. "How can I help you, Detective?"

"Just a few questions, Mrs. Wells. Have you worked at West Beverly Hospital long?"

"Almost ten years," she said.

"So, you knew Dr. Templeton well?"

She shook her head. "I didn't know him at all. I've always worked the night shift and you don't see plastic surgeons around here much at night. Most of our emergencies are more like appendicitis. Last night was the first time I'd ever seen Dr. Templeton."

"I see," Daniel said. "Do you remember what time it was when he first came into the recovery room?"

"Around midnight, I think. It was a few minutes before they brought the patient in."

"What did he do?"

"The usual. He wrote his orders, dictated his operative report, and made a call, probably to his exchange. I overheard him saying he was on his way home. When Dr. Venning brought the patient in, he talked to her, and to his patient, for a minute or two, and then he left."

"What time was that?" Daniel asked.

"I can't tell you exactly, but I think it was about ten past twelve, because I always do my vitals on the quarter hour, and he was gone when I took my first set of readings."

"Who was with the patient when she was brought in?" Daniel asked.

"Dr. Venning, of course, and the two O.R. nurses who wheeled her in on the gurney."

"Can you remember when each of them left?"

Martha shrugged. "Helen and Josie left right after they brought Miss Hayden back to recovery. Dr. Venning stayed around for about twenty minutes to be sure the patient was all right, and that there were no other cases for her. Then, she left too. That was after my second set of vitals, so I'd guess maybe 12:40 a.m."

"Did you see or hear anything out of the ordinary in the next hour?"

"No sir, it was pretty quiet."

"You've been a big help, Mrs. Wells. I'd like to ask you not to discuss the information you've given me with anyone else."

She nodded and left the room.

Daniel asked Brenda to check on all of Templeton's emergency cases for the past several years, and find out who was on staff those nights.

Just then, the phone intercom buzzed. It was Bill Pincus.

"Succinylcholine," he said.

"Succinyl what?"

"Succinylcholine, also known as anectine. It's a very powerful muscle relaxant used by anesthesiologists to paralyze patients prior to intubating them. It's a relative of curare. A high enough dose paralyzes the diaphragm in under a minute. Wesley was killed by an injection."

Daniel exhaled a low whistle. "So, the murderer had enough medical knowledge to know about this drug, had access to it, and was strong enough to hold onto him, while injecting it. Tall order."

"True," Bill said. "But it certainly eliminates any ninety-five pound weaklings. I can't wait for you to meet Dr. Venning."

"Don't you think that's a bit obvious?" Daniel asked. "If I were an anesthesiologist, I'd use something a little less likely to point right at me—rat poison for example."

"Remind me to stay in your good graces," Bill said.

CHAPTER FIFTEEN

DR. ADRIENNE VENNING WAS ABOUT FIVE-FOOT-TEN and built like a Vogue model. She had high cheekbones, sultry hazel eyes, and a mane of light brown hair, artfully highlighted with blond streaks. Even in scrubs, she was stunning.

Dr. Venning shook Daniel's hand, and slid gracefully into a seat.

"I heard the bad news," she said. "Is it really true that he was murdered?"

"I'm afraid so," Daniel said.

"How?"

"I can't divulge that information yet. I wonder if you could help us, by answering a few questions."

"Of course, but I don't know that I can give you any useful information. I didn't see or hear anything unusual."

"Had you worked with Dr. Templeton before last night?" Daniel asked.

"Yes, of course. He did a lot of surgery at West Beverly. I've given anesthesia for him, many times."

"Was he a good surgeon?" Daniel asked.

"Very," she said. "He was meticulous and thorough, very careful when patients had underlying medical problems, and he had a nice bedside manner with his patients. They all liked him."

"Did you like him?"

She hesitated a moment. "I liked working with him. He was thoroughly professional."

"What about on a personal level?" he asked. "Was he a nice guy?"

"I didn't know him very well personally, but I found him a little...slick. Too Beverly Hills, if you know what I mean."

"Did he ever make a pass at you?" he asked.

"Probably," she said. "Unfortunately, it seems to be an occupational hazard when you're a female anesthesiologist. Sexual banter is a surgeon's stock-in-trade. All they have to do is see a set of x chromosomes, and they develop a compulsion to let you know what studs they are. Wesley Templeton wasn't much different, in that regard, from any of his colleagues."

"Can you remember any specific incident? Did he make a pass at you last night?" Daniel asked.

She shook her head. "He seemed a little upset and preoccupied last night. Usually, he jokes a lot in the O.R. Last night, he was crabby. Kept snapping at the scrub nurse."

"When did you see him last?"

"In recovery. He finished his charting and left a few minutes past midnight. I stayed with the patient until I was sure she was stable. Then I went home."

"And what time was that?" Daniel asked.

"I got home around one so it must have been about 12:45 a.m., when I left the hospital. I don't live far away."

"Did you stop in the ladies' locker room, or see anyone else when you were leaving?" Brenda asked.

"No to both questions," she said. "I came in wearing scrubs. It saves me the bother of changing. The corridors and elevator were empty when I used them."

"Doctor," Daniel said. "Could you educate me about the drugs that are available on the operating room floor? Where are they kept and who has access?"

"You mean narcotic drugs?" she asked.

"Narcotics and other drugs used for anesthesia," he said.

She nodded. "Each anesthesiologist has a personal locked cart. It's usually kept fully stocked by the pharmacist, with everything except narcotics. Those are kept in a locked cabinet, to which only the charge nurse has the key. They have to be signed out and accounted for precisely during each case. The other drugs are kept in the pharmacy storeroom."

"Who has access to that?"

"Lots of people. The pharmacists are supposed to keep it locked if they leave the room, but I've seen it unattended."

"What drugs do you routinely keep on your cart?"

"I can give you a list if you wish. In general, I have local anesthetics, narcotics like demerol or versed, digoxin, epinephrine and anectine."

"What's anectine?" Daniel asked.

"We use it for muscle relaxation when we're inserting an endotracheal tube."

"When you locked your cart last night, was anything missing?" he asked.

She shook her head. "Not that I noticed."

"Was the cart locked while you were in recovery?"

"No, it wasn't. I locked it and put it away, just before I went home."

"Do you live alone, Doctor?" Daniel asked.

"I'm married," she said.

"And was your husband at home when you arrived last night?"

"At home and awake, Lieutenant. Am I supposed to need some kind of alibi?"

"Everyone who was here last night needs an alibi, Doctor," Daniel said. "Thank you for your help."

"She certainly had access to the drug, and the knowledge to use it," Daniel commented, after the doctor left. "But it appears as if just about anyone who knew the hospital could have had access. What we need is a motive."

"We'll find it," Brenda said. "Would you like me to check the pharmacy records and to count the remaining vials of anectine on her cart?"

He nodded.

His next witness was Helen Johnson, the circulating nurse. His first impression was of obesity so massive, he couldn't imagine how she circulated. She could barely stand. When he looked at her carefully, she seemed to be in her early forties, although he found age difficult to judge in heavy people. Her features were pretty but faded, and virtually lost in the chubby cheeks and massive double chin that obscured her neck. Short, blonde hair, with streaks of gray, was sprayed into careful submission.

She seated herself opposite Daniel, the huge rolls of her hips overlapping the sides of the chair, and folded her hands together over a stomach the size of a full-term pregnancy. She was breathing quickly, as if even the effort of seating herself had been too much for her overburdened cardiovascular system.

"I understand you want to ask me a few questions," she said, her face expressionless.

"I'm sure you've heard by now that Dr. Templeton was murdered last night, in the men's locker room," Daniel said. "We're questioning everyone who worked in the operating room that night."

"I heard," she said. "I hope you find the killer soon, or none of us will feel safe around here."

"When did you see Dr. Templeton last, Mrs. Johnson?"

"In the recovery room, after the case. Josie, the other nurse, helped me bring his patient in, and then we left to go home."

"What time?" Daniel asked.

"A little after midnight."

"And were you and Josie together after you left the recovery room?"

Helen hesitated. "Josie went back to the operating room to finish rinsing her instruments. I went to the ladies' locker room, changed clothes, and left."

"Did you see anyone at all, from the time you left Josie, to the time you reached your car?"

She shook her head.

"How well did you know Dr. Templeton?"

"I didn't know him at all. I just moved here two months ago. My husband's company transferred us and I've only been working evenings at West Beverly for the past few weeks. This was the first time I've done a case with Dr. Templeton."

"Thank you, Mrs. Johnson," Daniel said. "Let my sergeant know how we can reach you, if we need to talk to you again."

She braced her arms and hoisted herself out of the chair. "Certainly, Detective. Good luck."

Daniel waited until the door had closed before making a

comment. "Well, I doubt she killed him in a fit of jealous rage after he ended their passionate, illicit love affair."

"Don't make fun of fat people," Brenda said. "They have feelings too, and love affairs."

"You're right," he acknowledged. "One more nurse and we're through here."

He opened the door and asked the patrolman to bring in Josie Otero.

Miss Otero appeared to be from the Philippines, a short, small-boned, young woman with delicate features, devoid of make-up, and glossy black hair. She looked as if she'd been crying.

"Please sit down, Miss Otero." Daniel handed her a tissue and she accepted it gratefully, dabbing at her down-cast eyes.

"I'm sorry," she said. "I just heard a few minutes ago. Dr. Templeton was such a nice man. He was always so kind to the nurses. I can't believe someone would want to kill him."

"I know," said Daniel. "It's always a terrible shock when someone we know becomes a victim. I won't keep you long, but it would help a great deal if you could answer some questions."

"Of course," she said, regaining her composure.

"I understand you left the recovery room with Mrs. Johnson, about midnight. Where did you go then?"

"I went into the O.R. for a few moments to finish my work, then I changed and went home."

"Did anyone come into the O.R. while you were there?"

"No."

"Did you happen to notice if the anesthesia cart was locked?" he asked.

"I'm sorry, I didn't look at the cart."

"What about after you left the operating room?" Daniel

asked. "Did you see Dr. Templeton or anyone else in the suite?"

"No, I didn't. It was very quiet. The halls were empty. The only person I saw was the security guard, when I left the building."

"Do you know what time it was when you left?"

"I didn't notice. I'm sorry, lieutenant. I'm not being very helpful."

"Not at all, Miss Otero. You're being very cooperative. I gather you liked Dr. Templeton."

"Very much," she said.

"Did you have a friendship or any kind of social relationship with him?"

"Oh, no," Josie said. "He wouldn't have been friends with someone like me. He knew all kinds of famous, important people. But he was very popular among the nurses. He'd always bring doughnuts or coffee cake when he operated here in the mornings. He almost never yelled, the way some of the other surgeons do."

"What about last night? Was he nice to you?"

She hesitated. "He was unusually short-tempered," she said. "It wasn't like him. But I guess everyone has a bad day."

"Thank you, Miss Otero. I have no more questions for the moment."

Well, he thought, all of that was minimally helpful. His next job would be to track down Hannah's old roommate, the ex-wife, Sara. First, however, he would call Hannah and see if she could meet him for dinner. He was starving and he missed her. Dinner would solve both problems.

Smiling, he reached for his cell.

CHAPTER SIXTEEN

W HEN I WALKED INTO CALIFORNIA PIZZA KITCHEN, Daniel was seated in a booth, nursing a cold drink. When he saw me, his face lit up and he greeted me with a hug that was much more suited to a bedroom than a restaurant.

"Yes, it was definitely murder," he said, as he tucked into his barbecue chicken pizza. "And no, I can't give you the details. They're still confidential. All I can tell you, is that after dinner, I'm going to interview your friend Sara."

"I feel guilty that I never called her before all this happened," I said. "She'll be surprised to hear from you."

"I've already called her," he said.

"You didn't tell her over the phone?"

"Of course not. I just said I was with the police and I needed to ask her a few questions about her former husband. She said she wasn't surprised. She figured he'd get himself in trouble with the police, sooner or later."

That sounded like the kind of bitter comment Sara would make. I started in on my salad.

"Can I come with you?" I asked. "It might help Sara to

have a friend present when she gets the news, and she knows a great deal about Wesley. She might be more forthcoming with you if I'm there."

Daniel thought about that for a while.

I could see the conflict between doing things by the book, and potentially getting more information from Sara, as he mentally debated the pros and cons. Finally, information won out.

On the way to Santa Monica, I briefed Daniel on everything I could remember about Sara and Wesley's bitter divorce.

"Well, she certainly has a motive," Daniel said. "I guess we'll find out if she has an alibi."

"You don't seriously consider Sara a suspect, do you? Bitter as she is, she's far too ethical to commit murder."

"You know better than that, Hannah," Daniel said. "Don't let your friendship blind you to the possibility. The most gentle, ethical person in the world can be provoked to kill. If someone threatened your life, or Zoe's, even you could."

I knew he was right and it terrified me. Some part of me refused to seriously consider the possibility that Sara had done it.

The woman who answered the door was a mature version of the old Sara. Her hairdresser had restored the gray locks to an acceptable shade of brown, and her hair was drawn back and pinned with a black velvet bow. She was wearing a pair of navy blue slacks and a neatly pressed white blouse.

"I know you weren't expecting to see me," I said, forestalling her questions. "Detective Ross is a good friend and he let me come with him."

"So, what did he do?" she asked, as she led us into the living room. "Embezzle the hospital building fund?"

I shook my head. "Better sit down, Sara. I have some shocking news for you."

Sara sat down, looking confused.

"Wesley's dead," I told her. "He was murdered last night at West Beverly Hospital."

Sara's mouth fell open. "So, there is a fairy godmother after all."

She turned toward Daniel. "My ex-husband deserved to die, lieutenant. I'm not hypocritical enough to pretend I'm sorry he's dead. The only thing I'm sorry about is that someone beat me to it. Do you know who killed him?"

"We thought perhaps you could help us with that," Daniel said. "Could you tell us where you were last night?"

"Here," Sara said. "All night. I was working on some papers. I was taking Wesley back to court next week to increase my alimony and I was trying to get ready. I'm afraid I don't have any witnesses for you."

"Can you think of anyone who would want your husband dead?"

"To know him was to detest him. I'm sure there's a line of suspects around the block. What about his present wife? I'm sure by now he's got a new mistress. Maybe she found out about her?"

"Are you certain he was having an affair? Do you have any evidence?" Daniel asked.

"I was married to him. I know his character. Wesley could never settle for just one of anything."

"What about business associates?" Daniel asked. "Do you know about any business deals gone sour?"

"My husband was always doing shady deals and border-line investments. He loved sleazy tax shelters and running all his personal expenses through his practice. He thought it was his mission in life to outwit the IRS. I don't know who he currently deals with, but I'm sure you'll find something illegal. You might try talking with his accountant or with Mort Levine, his partner."

"Tell me about Dr. Levine. Did they get along?"

Sara shrugged. "Levine was good to Wesley when he first started practice. He took him under his wing, gave Wesley all the overflow, taught him the business end of private practice. He made him a thirty percent partner the second year, and let me tell you, thirty percent of that practice was a tidy bundle, but nothing was ever enough for Wesley. He was always complaining that he deserved a bigger wedge of the pie. The truth was, it would have taken him years to earn that much if he'd gone out on his own."

"Sara, you realize there won't be any alimony now. Can you support yourself? Is there some life insurance to help you?" I asked.

She nodded. "It was part of our dissolution agreement. He paid the premiums. I owned the policy. I'll get five hundred thousand dollars. That should support me for a while. I can't believe I can actually pick up my life again. I've spent the past four years on this divorce."

"Were you familiar with the physical layout at West Beverly Hospital?" Daniel asked.

Sara nodded. "I had a job there when we first moved to Beverly Hills. I was a staff psychologist in their chemical dependency unit, but I was only there two years. Wesley insisted I quit, so I could supervise the construction of our new house. Wesley sabotaged me every time I got started anywhere, professionally. I would have had a life by now, if I hadn't married him."

Daniel listened, sympathetically. I'd heard it all before, ad infinitum. I didn't think there was much more we could learn here at the moment, but I decided to invite Sara to go out to dinner with me later in the week. She might have more to offer if Daniel wasn't there, and I was determined to extract all the information she had. The best way to prove my old roommate wasn't a killer was to catch the person who was.

"So, now where to?" I asked Daniel, as we walked back to his car.

"I'll drop you off in Westwood, so you can pick up your car and head home. I've probably got another few hours of paperwork down at the station."

"Poor baby. If you don't mind having a Watson tag along, I'm free all weekend. I'm interested in hearing the rest of your interviews. We could start the morning's work with homemade waffles at my place."

Daniel stopped at a red light and leaned over to kiss me gently on the lips. I could tell how tired he was. "I'm afraid the department doesn't allow me to have a Watson, but I'd love some waffles. I've set up an early appointment with Dr. Levine. Do you mind having breakfast at seven-thirty?"

Oh, well, I'd tried. Early wasn't my favorite time for Saturday breakfast, but I'd manage. Zoe adored helping me make waffles.

CHAPTER SEVENTEEN

IT WAS SEVEN-THIRTY IN THE MORNING. ZOE, AUNT Jemima and I were making waffles in the kitchen when the phone rang.

"Hi, how are you?" It was a male voice, deep and rich, the sort of voice that belongs to the heartthrob on *Days of Your Lives*.

"Who is this?" I asked.

"It's Eddie."

"Sorry, Eddie. You've got the wrong number."

"Oh, no. I'm certain I have the right number. Tell me what you're doing right now?"

I slammed the phone down. All I needed was breakfast with a masturbatory telephone pervert. The phone rang again. *Damn it.*

"Hello!"

Silence and a click.

I hung up.

It rang a moment later.

I ended the connection, put my ringer on silent and my

phone machine on loud, just in case someone phoned whom I actually wanted to talk.

Like most physicians, I had an unlisted number. I'd hoped the caller had dialed it by accident and would forget it, but apparently, he either had a good memory or had written it down.

The smell of smoke assaulted my nostrils and I rescued a burnt waffle from the iron, just as Daniel rang the front doorbell. Zoe, still in her pajamas, let him in.

"Could we play Cinderella?" she asked. "You be Cinderella and I'll be the Prince."

Daniel raised an eyebrow. "I'd rather be the fairy godmother," he said.

"Then you be Cinderella, Mommy."

"Sorry," I said. "I'm not very good at housework."

I was pleased to see that Zoe had already figured out who got to have all the power and all the fun in life. She was very popular with her girlfriends because they never fought over the namby-pamby princess roles. Zoe was the kind of kid who wouldn't be caught dead in a dress, and liked to go trick or treating dressed as Tyrannosaurus Rex or a knight in shining armor. I figured she'd probably go to business school and wind up as a CEO somewhere.

I accepted a kiss from an exhausted-looking Daniel and handed him a large mug of black coffee. "You look like you had a late night."

"I did, and today is looking pretty busy as well."

I dished out waffles, fresh fruit salad and the maple syrup, and gave Zoe permission to eat her breakfast in front of the television set.

"So, Daniel," I asked, seating myself. "Who was in the operating room suite the night Wesley was murdered?"

"You know I'm not supposed to talk about ongoing cases."

"I'm not asking you to breach confidentiality. You've obviously never worked in a hospital. Trust me. The grapevine is better than Facebook. Every hospital employee probably knows the answer to that question. Besides, I've operated there and I know some of the staff. I might be helpful."

He nodded, as he finished chewing his first bite of waffle. "The anesthesiologist was a Dr. Venning. There was a scrub nurse named Josie Otero, a circulator, Helen Johnson, and a recovery room nurse, Martha Wells."

"I know Adrienne Venning. She's done cases for me. Nice woman and excellent anesthesiologist."

"She's also a knockout," Daniel said. "Do you think she's Wesley's type?"

"Do you mean, do I think they might have had an affair?"

Daniel nodded.

"Hard to say. She is gorgeous, but she's also very smart and independent. He might have viewed her as a professional rival. Don't forget, he married his office manager."

"Do you know any of the nurses?" Daniel asked.

"I'm afraid not. I usually operate during the day and they're probably evening shift."

Daniel finished the rest of his breakfast. "I'm interviewing Levine this morning. Then, I'm going to see what loose ends need following up. I'll call you if I get any free time."

I planted a kiss on his cheek and walked him to the door. Zoe and I were going to have a mother-daughter day, and then I was going to see if I could add to Daniel's sources of information. I watched him start his car and head north, to the fancy section of Brentwood.

CHAPTER EIGHTEEN

THE LEVINE HOUSE WAS IN AN AREA CALLED Brentwood Park, a few blocks north of Sunset. It was a tree-shaded district of two-acre lots and old money, less flashy, and to Daniel's mind more desirable than Beverly Hills. Although Hannah lived only ten minutes away, it was a different world. The house itself was a dramatic wood and glass contemporary, in a setting of large trees, informal garden and a private tennis court surrounded by tall hedges. When Daniel pulled up and parked, Brenda was waiting for him.

Dr. Levine greeted them, dressed in tennis whites and Nikes. Daniel estimated his age at about sixty, but he was fit, tanned, manicured and exquisitely barbered.

"Please come in," he said, shaking their hands. "I was just finishing my coffee outside."

He led them through a wall of glass doors onto a spacious brick patio, facing the pool. An attractive blonde, in her late thirties, was reading the Los Angeles Times on a chaise lounge. She was also dressed in tennis clothes.

"This is my wife, Ashley. Darling, this is Detective Ross

and Sergeant Jordan. They're here to talk about Wesley's horrible death."

Ashley looked up and rose to shake hands. "I still can't believe something like this could happen to someone we know. It's like a nightmare," she said.

"I know," Daniel said. "We all would like to think that murder is something that happens only to faceless strangers."

"You needn't stay, dear," Levine said. "The lieutenant can get all the information he needs from me. If he has any questions for you, I'm sure they'll keep until later."

He looked questioningly at Daniel, who nodded, and Ashley excused herself. Levine sat down, refilled his coffee from a porcelain pot, and offered them a cup. They declined.

"So, lieutenant, how may I be of help?"

"When was the last time you saw your partner, doctor?" Daniel asked.

"He saw patients in the office Thursday afternoon. I left before he did, about five o'clock. Ashley and I were meeting some friends for dinner and a concert at the Dorothy Chandler."

Daniel admired the casual way he'd slipped in his alibi.

"Did you go directly home after the concert?" he asked.

Levine shook his head. "We stopped for dessert and coffee at the Hyatt. Got home about one-thirty."

"I'll need to get the names and contact information for your friends, before we leave."

"Of course," Levine said.

Daniel continued. "Did Dr. Templeton mention anything to you about his plans for that evening?"

"Nothing special. We were both rather busy and didn't really talk much." He leaned back in his chair and crossed his right leg precisely over his left. It was almost as if he were trying to show how casual and unconcerned he was about their questions.

"Would you say that Wesley was a happily married man?" Brenda asked.

"He seemed content in his second marriage," Levine said. "I'm sure you know the first one ended in an acrimonious divorce."

"I understand he was having an affair with his second wife, while she was employed in your office," Daniel said.

"You may be right," Levine said. "But he was very discreet. I had no idea at the time."

"What about recently?" Daniel asked. "Did you have any reason to suspect he might have been involved with another woman?"

Levine shrugged. "He was very attractive to women. I suppose it's possible, but if so, I have no idea who she was."

"What about his business dealings? I understand there had been some talk between you of ending the partnership," Daniel said.

Levine's lips tightened. "That is true, lieutenant. I may as well give you this information since you will probably unearth it in any case, and I can save you the cost of an audit. I have recently discovered that, while Mrs. Templeton was employed as our office manager, she and Wesley embezzled close to one hundred thousand dollars from the practice."

"How?"

"It was very cleverly done. They opened a second PSA account, in both their names, at our bank."

"PSA?" Daniel asked.

"Plastic Surgery Associates, the name of our partnership. They ordered an endorsement stamp identical to the one we already had, but with the new account number on it. The patients were credited for their payments, but their checks were stamped with the new stamp. Then, when the deposits were made, one or two deposits each week would wind up in the wrong account. Since Erica did the bookkeeping, she simply failed to record those particular deposits."

"When did you discover all this?" Daniel asked.

"Just recently. Erica continued in her job, even after she and Wesley were married, but having the doctor's wife be the office manager became increasingly uncomfortable for the rest of the staff. We persuaded her to retire about six months ago. She made a few careless mistakes, during her last few weeks, that alerted my accountant. In any case, my lawyer was planning to institute proceedings to dissolve the partnership."

"What about filing criminal charges?" Daniel asked.

"We were considering that too, but I was hoping to avoid the negative publicity if the situation could be resolved privately."

Generous of him, Daniel thought. Well, Wesley's murder had certainly relieved him of the tedious task of dissolving the partnership. On the other hand, it would make it more difficult to retrieve his hundred thousand. He found it hard to believe that Levine was naive enough to have missed an affair going on under his nose. Or did he simply want to be perceived as naïve, so that the police wouldn't suspect some other motive. Maybe Wesley's roving eye had moved in the direction of Ashley. Sara certainly had been right when she said there wouldn't be any shortage of motives.

He verbalized those thoughts to Brenda as they returned to their cars.

"I agree, he's certainly got a motive," Brenda said. "But so far, he also seems to be the only player with a solid alibi."

"Maybe so, but don't rule him out," Daniel said. "He's got motive, knowledge and access to the drug. He also has the financial resources to hire someone to do the job."

"There's something that doesn't fit," Brenda said. "Erica told us Wesley received a call from the hospital at seven-thirty, but the patient didn't arrive at the emergency room until an hour later. I called the exchange when I got back to the station and the operator checked her logbook for me. Apparently, a woman called and said West Beverly Hospital was on the line for the doctor. She didn't give her name, or the operator didn't note it. I had someone double-check with all the nurses who were in the emergency room and the operating suite at the time, but no one admits to making the call. I also double-checked the ER sheet. It confirmed Miss Hayden wasn't brought in until an hour later."

"Interesting," Daniel said. "Good catch."

"Thanks," Brenda said. "Another thing. According to the housekeeper, Mrs. Templeton received a call the night of the murder, from a man. Gladys didn't know who he was, but he called about nine-thirty. She brought Mrs. Templeton some tea in her room at approximately ten o'clock and retired for the night. She claims to have slept until seven the next morning and not heard anything else. Her room is in a wing at the other end of the house from the garage, so Erica could have left the house and returned without anyone knowing. Also, you asked me to follow up on the blue Honda that was parked across the street from the house. It belongs to a downtown PI named Tommy DeLong. He's a small-time operator who does divorce work."

"No kidding," Daniel said. "I wonder which one of the Templetons hired him? Looks like we need to take a drive to his office."

CHAPTER NINETEEN

Tommy DeLong's office was on 9th and Olive, one of the seedier areas of downtown. Daniel had phoned ahead, presenting himself as an anxious client, and DeLong had agreed to meet them, even though it was Saturday morning.

"What if he won't talk to the police?" Brenda asked.

"I'll get a search warrant if we have to, but my bet is that he won't want the police on his back if he can avoid it."

They actually got a spot on the street, next to a meter with time on it. The building was 1930s, with some interesting deco touches but dingy. They took a creaky elevator to the fourth floor and entered the waiting room to DeLong's office. It was furnished with three straight-backed brown leather chairs, whose seats had seen better days. Gold, flocked wallpaper and matching carpet from the 60s completed the decor.

"Anybody home?" Daniel knocked on the inner door and it was rapidly opened.

DeLong's consultation room would have done well as a stage set for a Raymond Chandler novel, but DeLong himself would never have made it out of central casting. He was a short, pudgy man in his fifties, with a shiny bald, head surrounded by an untidy fringe of gray. Add another twenty years and a few pounds, and he'd fit right into a pinochle game in Miami.

"What can I do for you folks?" He ushered them indoors. A small electric fan moved the stale air and rustled an untidy pile of papers on a scratched wooden desk.

"You can tell us what you were doing Friday, parked outside the home of Wesley and Erica Templeton," Daniel said.

"Who wants to know?"

Daniel took out his police ID, and passed it across the desk.

DeLong picked it up and studied it. "Sorry detective. Consider it attorney-client privilege."

Daniel shook his head. "Afraid not, DeLong. First of all, you're not an attorney. Secondly, this is a murder case, and finally, I *will* get a search warrant for your office. You can tell me what I need to know, or I will tear this place apart looking for it, and question you down at headquarters. It's up to you."

"Jesus. You cops never give a guy a break, do you?"

"Not in a murder case," Daniel said.

DeLong hefted his body out of his chair, pulled a thin folder out of a file cabinet and tossed it over.

"I don't know anything about a murder," he said. "Erica Templeton hired me a week ago to tail her husband. She thought he might be getting some nookie on the side."

"And was he?" he asked.

"Not that I saw. Most of the time I tailed him from home, to the office, and back, except for Thursday night."

"Where was he on Thursday?" Daniel asked.

"He left the house about seven-thirty and drove to Spago. Looked like he had a reservation, because they seated him right away. I followed him in and had a few drinks at the bar. He seemed to be waiting for someone. Kept checking his watch and looked pretty pissed when they didn't show. I snuck a peak at the reservation list. He'd definitely reserved a table for two. Anyway, about eight-thirty, he called the waiter over and ordered. About nine o'clock, his beeper went off. He answered it with a little cellular phone. Kept it in one of those faggy-looking men's shoulder bags guys wear around Beverly Hills. Then, he paid his bill and left. I followed him to West Beverly Hospital and kept an eye on his car, waiting for him to leave. He never did."

"Did you, by any chance, convey any of that information to Mrs. Templeton?" Brenda asked.

"I called her about nine-thirty to tell her that he was at the hospital, and to find out if she had any further instructions. She told me to watch and see if he left with anyone. I was about to call one of my other operatives to take over in the morning, so I could get some sleep and some breakfast, when a bunch of cop cars arrived. I decided it would be a good idea to split. I had something to eat, and figured I'd drive by the Templetons' and report to my client. There were cop cars there, too."

"Where at West Beverly were you parked, Mr. DeLong?" Daniel asked.

"In the lot, one row behind Templeton's car. You know the setup. There's one big lot behind the hospital for doctors, employees and patients. Parking is free. There's no attendant."

"So, you must have seen everyone who arrived and left the hospital after you got there," Daniel said.

"Maybe so," DeLong said. "But, I wasn't paying much

attention to anyone but the guy I was tailing. I didn't know this was gonna turn into a murder case."

"Tell me everything you can remember about who went in and out," Daniel said.

DeLong shrugged. "It was a pretty quiet night. Around eleven, the night shift nurses arrived and the evening shift left. After that, I didn't notice anyone go into the place. Sometime between midnight and one, I noticed a few women leaving."

"Would you be able to identify any of them?" Daniel asked.

"There was one who was built like a whale and waddled when she walked. I might be able to recognize her. Otherwise, as I say, I wasn't paying much attention to any broad who wasn't with the doctor."

"Did you manage to see Mrs. Templeton Friday morning?" Brenda asked.

He shook his head. "I waited until the cop cars left and called her from my car. The housekeeper answered and said she couldn't talk to anyone, that Dr. Templeton had just passed away. I got the rest of the information on the six-o'clock news."

"Thanks," Daniel said. "You were very helpful. I'd better take this with me." He handed Brenda the file folder and she placed it in a sealed evidence envelope. "I'll call if I think of any more questions."

"You do that, detective." DeLong opened the door, and ushered them out with a slam.

"I wonder who she is," Brenda said, as she followed Daniel down the hall to the elevator.

"You mean the woman he was obviously supposed to meet at Spago?"

She nodded. "The one who called him at seven-thirty,

and provided an excuse for him to leave the house and meet her for dinner."

Daniel rang the button for the elevator and heard the cables creak as it came toward them. "I have the feeling that if we knew that answer, we'd be halfway to finding the killer."

"The problem with this case is that everyone with opportunity lacks motive, and vice versa. Now what?" Brenda said.

"Now, we go over the forensic evidence and see if there's anything helpful. Then we do background checks on everyone we interviewed. Maybe there's a connection we're not aware of yet."

Maybe he'd ask Hannah to have a private chat with her friend Sara. Even if Sara didn't do it, maybe she had a good idea of who did.

CHAPTER TWENTY

A HOMICIDE DETECTIVE ON THE TRAIL OF A KILLER IS a little like an obstetrician in the middle of a cesarean section—impossible to distract. Daniel did phone when he had a break, but he turned down my offer of dinner, promised me a rain check, and returned to the station house. He did, however, suggest that I might talk to Sara, and see if I could learn anything else that would be helpful. As I was planning to do that anyway, I agreed—in exchange for a few tidbits of additional information. So, Daniel filled me in on Wesley being stood up at Spago, by an unknown dinner companion. I wouldn't be surprised if the scumbag was there on a date. And if he was, I couldn't help thinking that it served his new wife right. Live by the sword, die by the sword.

I thanked Emilia, told her she was off for the evening, and took Zoe out for sushi. As soon as we got back, I tucked her in. Then, I reached for the phone and called my best friend Andrea. I hadn't had a chance to tell her about the murder, and I wanted her insight. I hoped that, somehow, she'd recognize something I'd missed. And I thought she might have some special insight into Wesley. Several years ago, during the worst of Sara's misery, I had recruited Andrea to become Sara's therapist.

Andrea was stunned when I told her that Wesley had been murdered.

"I know you can't tell me anything Sara told you in therapy," I said. "Even though I've probably heard it all anyway. But I'm hoping you might have some ideas about the killer."

I could hear Andrea exhale over the phone.

"You're going too fast for me," she said. "I've barely assimilated the fact that Wesley Templeton was murdered, and I'm not exactly a forensic psychiatrist. Why don't you tell me your analysis so far?"

I paused to collect my thoughts. "I've been pumping Daniel for information, but it hasn't been easy. He can't tell me everything. But, here's what I've put together. It seems to have been a crime of impulse and opportunity. No one could have known in advance that Wesley would be in the hospital that night. He didn't know himself, until he was paged. The weapon was a drug that just happened to be handy and deadly, at the same time. Daniel won't tell me what it is. The police are keeping that tidbit under wraps. So, I think we have a killer who decided to kill on the spur of the moment, and who's knowledgeable about drugs. That seems to narrow it down to one of the people who was in the operating suite that night, but none of them appears to have a motive."

"Unless, something happened that night that created a motive."

"Which is possible," I agreed. "There are three people

who might have motives. Erica, his wife, could have found out he was having an affair, although there is no proof of that yet. Levine, his business partner, was apparently going to end the partnership. Daniel implied some financial hanky-panky on Wesley's part. Then, of course, there's Sara, who despised him. Erica actually knew where he was, but it seems kind of far-fetched to me that she would have slipped into the hospital unseen, known which drug to obtain and what dose would be fatal, and taken the risk of ambushing him in the locker room. She could have killed him at home much more easily, and made it look like suicide or an accident.

"Levine, according to Daniel, apparently has an airtight alibi. Sara has no alibi at all, but the same argument applies to her as to Erica, with the additional proviso that she had no way of knowing where Wesley was. If she wanted to kill him, I can think of a dozen better ways to do it. You don't think Sara could have done it, do you?"

"Are you asking for a psychiatric assessment?" Andrea said.

"Yeah, I guess I am. I need it for my peace of mind. Can you give it, without breaching confidentiality?"

"I think so," Andrea said. "You have to understand that Sara has spent the past several years trying to make sense out of two decades of her life. She was married to a man who gaslighted her. He took control of her life and systematically destroyed her self-confidence, which is why, like any abused wife, she tolerated all those years of deprivation. She was too frightened, too insecure and too immobilized to get out.

"I agree with you that Sara doesn't seem like the type of woman to commit a murder. She's extremely ethical and also has a very rigid sense of morality. But finding out the truth, after all those years of abuse and neglect, could push anyone over the edge. The reason I think she's an unlikely suspect has to do with timing. She's so much better and happier now, than she was a few years ago. Why now, rather than when she was at the peak of pain and fury? It doesn't make clinical sense to me."

"I feel better," I said.

"What do *you* know about Wesley that might shed some light on who would want to kill him?" Andrea asked.

"The same things you know. He was a compulsive womanizer, who spent his married life having affair after affair. He was greedy, narcissistic and a thief. I suspect that if he stole from his partner, it wasn't the first time. He probably raided the cash register in the family grocery store when he was a kid."

"So," Andrea said. "It's likely that the killer was someone he stole from, or slept with, or both. It also seems likely to me that the killer was a woman. A lethal injection doesn't require a great deal of physical strength, and as you've mentioned, Wesley was the only man in the operating suite that night."

"Which means the killer knew that he'd be alone in the men's locker room," I said.

"Exactly. If I were you, I'd enlist some help from Sara. She might recognize a name, or photograph, of one of the women who were there that night."

"I was planning to do just that," I said. "I'm sure Daniel is already digging into their past histories. Perhaps, there's a place where one of their paths crosses Wesley's."

CHAPTER TWENTY-ONE

I PHONED SARA AND ARRANGED TO HAVE DINNER with her later in the week. Then, I curled up on my sofa and tried to remember back four years, to the aftermath of her split with her husband. Once she'd made contact with me, Sara had called constantly, updating me on each revelation that came from her meticulous review of twenty years of files.

"I cross-referenced his date books with the MasterCard bills for all his medical meetings," she said. "I called the hotels and got copies of his invoices. They're all double-rooms for Dr. and Mrs. Templeton. I never went with him—never. I tracked one invoice to a department store in Dallas. Mrs. Templeton bought a size ten dress at Neiman's. I wear a six, and I've never been to Dallas."

There was a lot more of the same. The impressive thing about it was that it was consistent over the years.

"How could you not suspect?" I kept asking her. "It never occurred to you once, in all those trips he made without you, that

there might be another woman? You knew he'd been unfaithful before."

"I loved him so much, and I had no one else to depend on. I wish to God, I'd had the sense to divorce him, the first time I caught him."

"Things could be worse," I said. "At least, you don't have children to fight over."

"I wanted children," she said. "I tried for years to get pregnant. He let me put myself through all kinds of infertility testing. Finally, I gave up and suggested we adopt. That's when he told me he'd had a vasectomy during residency and didn't want children. Can you imagine? Sterilizing himself and not even telling me?"

"You must have been furious."

"Unfortunately, I didn't get angry. I got depressed," she said. "So depressed, I took an overdose and wound up in the hospital. I just wanted to die. I was furious at Wesley for coming home and finding me before I did. It took me over a year to come out of that depression. That was another reason Wesley and I dropped out of sight. I didn't have any emotional energy to give to any of my friends."

I knew exactly how she felt. I didn't have much emotional energy to give either, and Sara was rapidly draining the little I had. Each phone call was a marathon, lasting a minimum of an hour and sometimes longer. Sara would ignore my subtler hints at ending the conversation, forcing me to resort to rudeness I would rather have avoided, or to depend on Zoe's shrieks for attention to rescue me.

For a while, I tried inviting Sara over for dinner, thinking it would do her good to socialize and be distracted by other people's lives. But each dinner turned into an endless, angry diatribe about Wesley the psychopath, and her barracuda lawyer, who was doing everything wrong. I kept trying to uncover Sara, my old roommate, with her funny stories, her warmth and her witticisms, but I couldn't find her. There was only a worn, middle-aged woman whose once beautiful face was contorted into expressions of rage. I felt powerless to help her, and resentful of her time demands. Then, suddenly, the phone calls stopped.

I was so relieved, it took me awhile to start worrying. By the time I got around to calling her, it was almost too late.

"Sara, did I wake you? What's wrong?"

Her speech was slurred and slow, as if each word was an effort. "I'm so glad you called."

She started to cry.

"What is it? You haven't taken any pills, have you?" My heart was in my mouth.

There was a long pause. "No, but I'm so scared. I want to die. Everything feels empty. I haven't been able to do anything for weeks."

"Have you been out of the house?" I asked.

"I don't think so. I can't remember."

"What are you doing for groceries?"

"The market delivers," Sara said. "I'm afraid to drive the car."

"Hang on," I said. "I'm coming over."

It took her forever to answer the door. She was in her nightgown, tearful and disheveled; cigarette butts in piles all over the living room.

"When was the last time you ate?" I asked.

She shook her head. "Don't remember. I've been sleeping most of the day."

She withdrew to a corner of the sofa and lit another cigarette.

The refrigerator was empty. I ransacked the kitchen, found a can of Campbell's, and heated it for her, spooning the soup into her mouth.

"Sara, you need help. We've got to get you a psychiatrist."

"I've been to psychiatrists. They don't help and they don't

know anything. They can't fill up the hole inside me." The hand holding the cigarette was shaking uncontrollably.

"Maybe not," I said. "But a good therapist can help you hang on long enough to begin to fill it up yourself."

Sara began crying again. "If I died, it would stop hurting. All this pain would go away."

"Finish your soup," I said. "I have a phone call to make."

I went into her study and phoned Andrea. Fortunately, it was Saturday and she was home.

"I don't know what to do," I said. "Sara's severely depressed and suicidal. If I leave her, she'll kill herself. She's tried before. I hate to impose on you, but I don't know where else to turn. Could you take her on as a patient?"

"It sounds like she may need to be hospitalized," Andrea said. "Why don't you bring her to my office and let me see her?"

"Give me an hour to get her dressed and mobilized," I said. "And thanks. You're the best."

I brought Sara to Andrea's and sat in the waiting room while they had their consultation. An hour later, Andrea came out and told me Sara had agreed to go to the hospital. I drove her to St. Agnes, a private psychiatric hospital on the Westside and guided her through the admissions paperwork. Then I returned to her house, to pack a suitcase for her, and notify her security service that she would be away.

"I don't know what I would have done without you," I said to Andrea. I had dropped Sara's things off at Andrea's house, so she could bring them in to her, when she made rounds the next day. "I'm sorry to hand you such a major problem."

"These kinds of problems are my job. It's what I do best. I'll try and help her, Hannah, but it's not going to be easy. She's very sick right now."

"I don't see how you can take care of people who are this depressed all the time. Don't they suck you dry?" I asked.

Andrea shook her head. "They're my patients, not my friends. I leave their pain in the office. I don't take it home with me. Or at least, that's the theory."

"I wish you could tell me how not to take it home with me."

"You need to withdraw from this situation," Andrea said. "You don't have the emotional wherewithal to let Sara lean on you all the time. You still haven't dealt fully with your own pain, and you've got a child who needs a happy mother."

Easy for her to say, but I knew it was the right advice. When Sara was discharged a month later, she was better, but still too depressed to call me. I swallowed my guilt and restrained the impulse to call her. After all, I'd left her in competent hands. The next time I saw her, it was to break the news of Wesley's murder.

CHAPTER TWENTY-TWO

Sara and I had agreed to meet at The Courtyard Kitchen, a little place on Montana that had great food and reasonable prices.

I called Daniel to let him know I was going to see Sara for dinner, and ask if he could obtain photos for me of everyone who was in the operating room that night.

"Anything new?" I asked.

"Only negatives. No fingerprints, no hair, no fibers, no secretions. I suspect the killer wore surgical gloves, and an operating room hat and shoe covers. We haven't found the syringe. The only thing we know for sure, is that one vial of the drug is missing from the anesthesia cart."

"Keep me posted," I said.

Sara was already at the table when I arrived, sipping a glass of red wine. She smiled and waved at me. I thought she looked better than at any time I'd seen her, since the breakup. It's remarkable how a good hairdresser can take ten years off your face.

"You look wonderful," I said, as I seated myself.

"I'm a free woman," she said. "I'll never have to deal with that bastard again. I've got my life back, and it feels great."

I didn't know how to respond to that. Somehow, it seemed inappropriate to be celebrating a murder, so I occupied myself with reading the menu instead.

"You haven't told me how you got involved in Wesley's murder," she said.

I collected my thoughts for a moment, while the waiter hovered over us, and I ordered the salmon. Sara asked for the roast lamb.

"Why should you care who killed Wesley?" she asked. There was a look on her face that seemed almost hostile.

"I guess I care, because the first thought that occurred to me when I heard about the murder, was that you would be on the list of suspects. I thought the quickest way to remove you from it was to find out who really did it."

"What made you so sure I didn't?" she asked.

I smiled at her. "I've known you for over twenty years. I know your character. You're not capable of murder."

Sara buttered a chunk of French bread. "You still haven't told me how you wound up in the middle of this."

"Detective Ross is a good friend. I don't know if you heard about Ben's sister Beth. It was in the Santa Monica papers about a year ago. She was murdered. Daniel handled the case."

Sara reached over the table and touched my hand. "I didn't know, Hannah. I'm so sorry. It must have been a nightmare for you. I remember meeting Beth. She was lovely."

I didn't want to talk about Beth again. I'd been obsessed with her death and was just beginning to put it behind me.

"Anyway," I continued. "Daniel and I started seeing each other. We were on vacation two weeks ago, and we ran into

Wesley. When the murder happened, Daniel told me about it."

"I see."

The food arrived and we turned our attention to it. Sara sliced her lamb into small, even pieces, chewing slowly and swallowing each mouthful with a sip of wine.

"There were four other people in the operating suite that night," I said. "All women. I brought some photographs with me. I was hoping you'd be willing to look them over, and see if anyone looks familiar to you."

Sara shook her head. "I don't want to be involved in this. I'm very grateful to whoever killed Wesley and I hope she gets away with it. Whoever she was, she probably had a good reason."

"You really hated him so much, you'd want to see his killer go free?" I asked.

"You bet. You don't know the half of it, Hannah. Did I ever tell you about Valerie?"

"Was she another woman he had an affair with?"

"Oh, no," she said. "It's much better than that. Valerie was his illegitimate child. She must be eighteen by now. She was born the year we were married. From the day of our wedding, he was screwing someone else."

"So, he had a child with another woman, and sterilized himself so he couldn't have one with you? Unbelievable. How did you find out about her?"

"I subpoenaed the contents of his safe deposit box before he got to it. It was full of letters from a woman named Ellie. One of them told him that their child, their Valerie, had just been born."

"I'm sorry, Sara. You're right. He was a shit. I understand if you don't want to get involved. In your place, I'd probably feel the same way."

"Thanks," Sara said. "I think I need some dessert. This place has the world's greatest toll house cookie pie."

We split the pie and ice cream and ordered coffee to go with it.

"Sara," I finally managed to say. "I just want you to know how badly I feel about disappearing from your life. It was just a bad time for me. You were so needy, that I couldn't keep up with you and take care of myself and Zoe at the same time. I'm sorry if I hurt you."

She smiled and shook her head. "You didn't disappear. You were there when I needed someone the most. If it hadn't been for you, I'd have probably killed myself. I understand how you felt. People who are as depressed as I was are awful to be around. I knew I was driving all my friends away. I just couldn't help it. Anyway, I'm glad you're back. I'll try to be more entertaining company."

Emilia was waiting to talk to me when I came back from dinner.

"He call again," she said.

"Who?"

"You know, that Eddie you tell me about. Zoe answer the phone. He say 'can I speak to your mommy,' so she give me the phone. He ask 'is *she* home?' Then he say lots of dirty things."

"Why didn't you hang up?" I asked. "These perverts love it when you talk to them."

"I not afraid of him. I tell him what he do not right and I tell him I going to call the police. I think he like your voice, Hannah."

"Great," I said. Just what I needed, a sex maniac who thinks I'm sultry.

I was more disturbed that Zoe had answered the phone. Who knows what he'd said to her, or what he might say, if he called again.

"Let the phone machine pick up the calls for a few days. Tell Zoe not to answer the phone. Maybe he'll get bored and fall in love with someone else."

CHAPTER TWENTY-THREE

I GOT HOME IN TIME TO PUT ZOE TO BED, AND TO indulge us both in a bedtime story and a long snuggle. Then, I retreated to my bedroom and called Daniel.

"Any luck with Sara?" he asked.

"Yes and no," I said. "She doesn't want to get involved. She refused to look at the photos. She thinks that if we catch the killer, we should pin a medal on her."

"You both think it's a woman?"

"Don't you? For one thing, there weren't any men in the operating suite."

"Was that the yes part?" Daniel asked.

"No. The yes part is much more interesting. It seems that, even while he was courting Sara and they were exchanging wedding vows, Wesley was having an affair with a woman named Ellie. They had an illegitimate daughter together, named Valerie. She's probably about twenty now."

"That *is* interesting. And worthy of a follow-up," Daniel said. "Thanks. Are you busy Saturday?"

"What do you have in mind?" I asked.

"The coroner's released Wesley's body to the family. The

services are going to be on Saturday. I thought it might be valuable to see who shows up. How about I take you to the funeral, and afterwards, I take you to bed? I'm off duty."

I gathered he'd caught up on his sleep. "I'm not on call either. Why don't we just skip the funeral?" I asked. "It's not my kind of foreplay."

"Sorry," Daniel said. "You've got to eat your vegetables before you get dessert."

Daniel was in his office, reviewing personnel files of everyone who'd been in the OR that night. The file on Dr. Venning contained a photograph, which looked as though it had been taken by a professional photographer. More like a cover shot for People Magazine, than a mug shot for an application. Adrianne's elegant face, with its tawny mane of hair, stared up at him. If Wesley had been sexually involved with any of the four women, surely it would have been the anesthesiologist. According to the application, she was thirty-three years old and married. Neither the name of her husband, nor the date of the marriage, were noted. She'd been born and educated in New York, and after completing her anesthesia residency, had spent two years at Darby Community Hospital in Connecticut. She'd moved to Los Angeles three years ago, obtained a California license and a job at West Beverly.

He wondered what her motive had been for abandoning her East Coast roots and moving west. A man, perhaps? He'd have to find out who her husband was and how long they'd been together. It seemed unlikely she'd known Wesley prior to moving to Los Angeles, but he wondered if she'd been the woman he'd been planning to meet at Spago.

Martha Wells's photo was ten years old. In the interim, her face had sagged and her hair had turned gray. According to her initial application, she was fifty years old. She had gone to nursing school at Martin Luther King Hospital in Watts. She'd worked there for four years, and then transferred to the surgical service at L.A. County, where she'd been a scrub nurse until 2000. At that point, she'd joined the staff at West Beverly.

He skimmed her work record. It appeared that Martha Wells had been well-liked, conscientious and had received favorable evaluations from all her nursing supervisors. The entire time she'd been employed at West Beverly, she'd worked the night shift, apparently by choice. The application noted that she was divorced and had two children. He did a rapid mental calculation and noted that Wesley had been at L.A. County Hospital from 1996-2000. Had Martha been lying when she said she'd never met him?

The third file belonged to Helen Johnson. It was slim, containing only an application form and a few letters of recommendation from her previous job. Helen was 41, married and had one child born in Maryland. She had gotten her B.A. from Boston University. Somewhere in the next few years, Helen had apparently moved west. She'd gone to nursing school at the University of Washington, in Seattle, and had obtained an R.N. She'd remained at the University Hospital, first as a surgical scrub nurse, and later as an operating room supervisor. Her references were all enthusiastic. It was an innocuous file, except for a five-year blank space, but he imagined that could be easily explained by "married, one child." Women didn't much like to put "housewife" on their resumes. Nevertheless, he made a mental note to find out about the missing years.

He turned to the final file on Josie Otero. Josie was 24,

single, and had been born in the Philippines. She'd attended Our Lady of the Perpetual Light High School and nursing school at St. Jude's Hospital in Manila. After graduating, she'd moved to Los Angeles and obtained her first job at West Beverly. Apparently, it was easier to obtain a green card if you were a trained nurse, so many young Filipinas had left home to seek success in Southern California. Her evaluations suggested she could use a little more self-confidence, but there were no complaints of any substance.

He replaced the files in his desk drawer, fixed himself some coffee, and tried to decide what to do next.

CHAPTER TWENTY-FOUR

W ESLEY'S FUNERAL WAS LIKE WESLEY'S LIFE —ostentatious. It was a large affair at Forest Lawn, in an air-conditioned chapel, packed with close to two hundred people. Most of the women were expensively dressed and had perfect noses and jaw lines. I labeled them patients. I knew there were several plainclothesmen in the audience, taking discreet photos with hidden cameras, and the sign-in book would be confiscated at the end of the service.

Daniel scanned the crowd for familiar faces. He pointed out Mort and Ashley Levine, who were seated, stone-faced, at the back of the room. Sara was conspicuously absent, nor did he initially spot any of the nurses from the operating room. There was a closed coffin of polished mahogany, draped with wreaths of flowers, sitting on the stage dais. A minister, who obviously hadn't known Wesley from a hole in the wall, talked about his life as a compassionate and beloved physician, his loyalty to family and friends, and his standing in the medical community. Sara would have puked.

The last funeral I'd been to was Beth's. I'd been numb with pain and cried my eyes out. This time, I watched with the detachment I'd feel at a movie. I couldn't bring myself to hurt for Wesley's loss. Not after the way he'd treated Sara.

At the end of the service, the crowd was instructed to reassemble at the graveside, after which, Mrs. Templeton would be receiving close friends at the family home. Daniel and I stood at the back of the chapel watching the crowd file out, some heading toward their cars, the remainder begin ning the walk up the hill. Erica, dressed in a well-cut black suit and hat, her face veiled, led the procession. Toward the back of the crowd, Daniel spotted a woman he identified as Josie Otero. She looked thin and vulnerable, in a sleeveless, navy blue summer dress, and from the quick glimpse I had of her childlike face, she seemed to have been crying.

"Can we go now?" I whispered.

Daniel nodded. "My place?"

I shook my head. It was two in the afternoon and Zoe wasn't due home from her play date until six. I planned on feeding them both, putting Zoe to bed, and curling up with Daniel for a quiet evening at home. I was sure I could think of something to do between the time we got to my place and Zoe's return.

It was a Santa Ana day, and the ambient temperature at Forest Lawn was at least one hundred. The interior of Daniel's car was like a blast furnace. It took a while to get comfortable, even with the air conditioner going. I was wearing a black linen dress with a pair of sandals. Daniel got onto the Ventura freeway, humming as he drove, both of us feeling increasingly better as we left the morbid atmosphere of the cemetery and headed home. As we reached the 405 and started south over the hill, Daniel took a hand off the wheel and started caressing my thigh, working my skirt gradually upward, until he found bare skin. I opened my legs, letting my fingers trail along the back of his hand, while I kept a careful eye on the road. I had this almost irresistible impulse to unzip him and do something outrageous in the car. It was hard to believe that after five years of ignoring sex, I could barely go two weeks without it. I felt like a horny teenager.

We found a parking spot across the street from my condo and a blast of cool air greeted us as I opened the door. I wondered what Daniel would like first, my body or a Coke.

"Cold drink?" I asked. No well brought-up girl ever forgets to offer refreshments to a guest. My mother would probably have whipped up a chicken sandwich to go with it.

"Love one," he said, collapsing on the sofa.

I went into the kitchen, filled a glass with ice cubes and poured the drink. I handed it to him, kissed the top of his head, and excused myself to go upstairs for a moment.

Now that we were actually going to make love at my house, I found myself feeling anxious. Usually, we went to Daniel's place, where neither privacy, nor my memories of Ben, were an issue. I went into the bathroom, washed my face, put on some blush and ran a comb through my hair. Then I checked my bedroom to be sure I hadn't left it looking like a bomb went off.

The bed was actually made and only a few odd pieces of underwear were lying on the carpet. I tossed them into my laundry hamper. Ben's photo was sitting in its usual place on my desk. It had put quite a damper on Daniel's and my first, abortive attempt to become lovers. I picked it up and stared at it. Ben had always been a very generous and loving husband. If there was an afterlife, he was probably up there telling me it was okay to do this. I opened a drawer and slipped the frame into it, face down. When I looked up, Daniel was standing at the bedroom door, watching.

"Does that mean I'm allowed to come in?" he asked, glancing in the direction of my desk.

I nodded.

He held out his arms for me and I made a beeline for them, stretching myself along the length of his body, inhaling the faint scent of aftershave, and feeling the taut muscles of his chest and legs.

"You have no idea how much I've missed this," he said, reaching behind me to unzip the dress.

I let it drop to the floor. "Me too. You addicted me when we were on vacation."

"This kind of addiction is good for you. It makes your skin glow." He unhooked my bra and took one of my nipples in his mouth.

I closed my eyes and gave myself up to the pleasure of it.

His hands were stroking my back with long gentle strokes that made my skin tingle.

I unbuttoned his shirt, undid his belt buckle and reached inside, teasing him with my fingertips.

"A woman with no patience," he said, finishing the job of undressing us.

"Not one of my virtues," I said. "But, I do have others."

"I've noticed." He scooped me up in his arms and carried me over to the bed.

I felt a little like Scarlett O'Hara being swept up the staircase, only I was certain I outweighed her by fifty pounds. Daniel didn't seem to be having a problem.

He grinned at me, as he set me down and kissed me. "I've always wanted to do that."

I reached up and pulled him down to me.

This time there were no ghosts in the bedroom.

CHAPTER TWENTY-FIVE

"WHAT TIME DOES ZOE COME HOME?" DANIEL asked. I rolled over and looked at the clock. We'd been napping for over an hour.

"At six," I said. "We should get up in a few minutes."

Daniel drew me closer and started covering my face with little kisses.

"Don't start," I warned. "We don't have time to do it again."

"Would it throw you into a panic if I said I was starting to fall in love with you?"

I thought about it for a minute.

"Not a complete panic," I said. "Just a very small anxiety attack."

I kissed him back.

"You are a very special man. And you're doing an outstanding job of battering down my defenses. Keep it up."

"Actually," Daniel said. "If the truth be told, I could take you or leave you, but I'm head over heels about Zoe."

I threw a pillow at him, and followed it with the pile of clothes he'd left on the floor.

"What are we making for dinner?" he asked.

"Pizza," I said. "Now where did I put my cell?"

Zoe was dropped off at home promptly at 5:45 p.m., and she greeted me with a hug that was only marginally more enthusiastic than the one she gave Daniel.

"I made you a book, Mommy," she said, handing me an elaborate collection of colored construction paper.

The title said *About Land by Zoe.* The first page showed a kangaroo in conversation with a butterfly. The next pages were illustrated with water, grass and rainbows. The final page showed two stick figures, hugging. Zoe had written, "Land has Love."

"That's Mommy and Zoe," she said.

My eyes started to tear, and I passed the book on to Daniel.

"Smart daughter you have," he said.

Pizza Man chose that moment to deliver, and we all sat down to one of my more wholesome and nutritious meals.

"I have a great idea, Mommy," Zoe said. "I think Daniel should have a sleepover date at our house."

Daniel was smiling from ear to ear.

"That's a nice suggestion, honey," I said. "But where would we put him?"

She thought about it for a while. "I could sleep with you, and Daniel could have my bed."

Daniel's face fell slightly.

I flashed him a malicious grin. "That's very generous of you Zoe, but I think your bed's too small for Daniel. Maybe we could put him on the sofa."

"That's a great idea, Mommy. Can you stay?" she asked Daniel.

"I think so," he said.

I made a mental note to do something especially nice for my daughter.

~

We put Zoe to bed, closed the doors to both bedrooms, and made love again. I had one ear open the whole time, but Zoe slept through. She really is a remarkably good child.

"I'd better go downstairs before I fall asleep," Daniel said. "I know you're not ready to have Zoe find us in bed together."

I snuggled closer and put my head on his shoulder. It was about midnight.

"Zoe wakes up at seven," I said. "She's like a little alarm clock. I promise I'll get you up in time."

"You're the boss," he said.

As it turned out, I didn't need to worry about getting him up at six. I woke up like a shot at two a.m. to a horrible noise that sounded like my security alarm. My heart was pounding.

"Relax, it's just my beeper," Daniel said. He reached down to his side of the floor, located his pants, and silenced the thing. I handed him the phone.

"This is Detective Ross," he said. "I thought I was off duty. What's wrong?"

I watched him as he listened and nodded.

"Give me the address," he said.

I handed him a pad and a pencil.

His face was looking grim and serious as he took down

the information, a poor prognosis for a romantic Sunday breakfast.

"What happened?" I asked, as he hung up the phone.

"Bad news," he said. "Josie Otero is dead."

CHAPTER TWENTY-SIX

D ANIEL DRAGGED HIMSELF OUT OF BED, GROANING, and attempted to collect his clothes off the floor.

I went down to the kitchen and made him a cup of coffee for the road.

"I'm sorry about this, honey," he said. "I was really looking forward to spending Sunday with you and Zoe."

"Me too," I said. "What happened to Josie? Was she murdered?"

"I don't know yet. She didn't show up for work and she didn't answer the phone. Finally, someone at the hospital asked the manager of her apartment complex to check on her. He found her and called the cops. Brenda was on duty and recognized Josie's name from the Templeton files. She thought there might be a connection, so she sealed the place, sent for the forensic team and phoned me."

I walked him to the door.

"Call me later and tell me what happened," I said.

"I will," he promised, "but it may be late. You know what it's like if it does turn out to be murder."

I kissed him goodbye, double-locked my door and

armed the security system. I felt a chill work itself down my spine. Somehow, I couldn't imagine that Josie's death was just a coincidence.

I tossed and turned my way back to sleep, only to be jolted awake at four a.m. by the telephone.

"Daniel?" I asked, picking up the receiver.

"It's me, Eddie."

I slammed down the phone, heart pounding, and turned the lights on. It was then that I realized he'd called on my back-line, the one I have so my exchange can reach me in an emergency. This was serious. It meant he knew who I was and somehow had access to both of my unlisted numbers. I tried to remember who else had my emergency number. The exchange, of course, Labor and Delivery, the medical staff office, Ruth, Zoe's school office—that was it.

My primary number was all over town. By now, I'd undoubtedly given it to every take-out restaurant in Brentwood. But I never gave people the back-line. I had a horrible vision of Eddie, whoever he was, sitting in his car, parked across the street, calling from a cellular phone. I made my way into the kitchen and found my knife drawer, selecting the largest one I owned. Then I went into the darkened living room and peered through the crack in the drapes. The street seemed quiet. None of the cars, that I could see, seemed to have an occupant.

I returned to my bedroom and put the knife in the drawer of my bedside table. Then I checked to be sure Zoe was still asleep, and turned on the television. There was no way I was going to get any more sleep tonight. On Monday, I'd call the phone company and change my unlisted numbers.

Zoe awakened at seven, ready to play. I put on my jeans, took her out for pancakes, and waited for a semi-civilized hour before making rounds at L.A. Memorial. Zoe used to enjoy coming on rounds, but lately she went with me under protest. I guess the novelty of watching Mommy take staples out of surgical incisions had begun to pall. When we got home, I called Andrea.

"What are you doing for lunch?" I asked.

"Leftover lasagna," she said. "Did you want to make me a better offer?"

"Zoe's got a birthday party from twelve to three," I said. "How would you like to have Sunday lunch at Spago?"

Spago was one of those permanently trendy Los Angeles restaurants where celebrities hopped from one good table to another, and ate duck sausage with pistachios at Tiffany prices. Sunday lunch wasn't a particularly popular time, and we were in the middle of a recession, so I was able to get reservations without much trouble. They did put us in the less fashionable back room but I could live with that. Andrea ordered the seared scallops and potato vegetable tortellini with saffron, tomato and black-olive sauce, and I nibbled on grilled, free-range chicken, while I brought her up to date.

"So, what are we doing hanging around here with the rich and famous?" she asked.

"I thought it might be nice to have a talk with the maître d'," I said. "Wesley was dining here the night he was killed and someone stood him up. Perhaps this was one of his regular places. Maybe someone will remember seeing him with a blonde."

"It's kind of a crowded restaurant," Andrea said. "Why would they remember him?"

"Wesley was the kind of guy who always liked to get VIP treatment. He was constantly chatting up the waiters whenever we went out to dinner with him. I suspect that if he came here regularly, he'd have made certain they knew him."

Our waiter appeared with two large cups of cappuccino, followed by the maître d', who was making the rounds, asking if everything was to our satisfaction.

I flashed him my most charming smile.

"Lunch was perfect," I said. "I wonder if I might have a word with you for a few moments."

"Of course, madam." He bent toward me.

"I'm Dr. Kline with West Beverly Hospital. One of our medical staff was dining at Spago about ten days ago. Shortly afterward, he was murdered. You may have read about it. We thought you might have some information that could be helpful."

"I assume you are referring to the unfortunate death of Dr. Templeton," he said. "I saw it in the paper. He dined here regularly."

Andrea flashed me a look of admiration.

"Did he dine with any particular companion?" I asked.

"The doctor liked beautiful women," he said. "I don't know the names of any of his companions, but the past few times he was here, he was with a very attractive brunette."

That eliminated Ashley Levine. Erica perhaps?

"About forty?" I asked. "Tall, very thin, flat-chested, narrow long face?"

He shook his head. "Definitely not flat-chested, Madame, a lovely young woman, in her twenties I would guess."

"Did they seem affectionate?" Andrea asked.

"I really can't say," he said. "This is a very busy restaurant. I escort patrons to their tables. I don't have time to watch what they do once they're seated."

"Did Dr. Templeton have a regular table?" I asked.

The maître d' shook his head. "No, but he did prefer the back room. The front room is for people who want to be seen."

"Perhaps there might be a waiter who remembers him?" I suggested.

The waiter's name was Tom, and he'd served Wesley the night of his death, and at dinner three weeks before. It must have been just prior to the Templetons' Carolina vacation. Tom had the kind of looks that made you suspect he was planning to make it big in Hollywood, just as soon as some major studio had the good sense to discover him.

"Nice guy," Tom said. "Always friendly, big tipper."

"You wouldn't happen to know the name of the young woman who was with him?" I asked.

He shook his head. "She was a looker, though. I saw him feel her up under the table, while they were eating."

"So, you would say they knew each other intimately?" Andrea said.

"Better than that," Tom said. "You couldn't blame him. She was something special."

"What about the last night he was here?" I asked. "Do you know if the same woman was supposed to meet him?"

Tom nodded. "He told me he was expecting his young lady. Seemed pretty ticked off when she stood him up."

"Just one more question," I said. I had just thought of another brunette possibility. "Was the woman Caucasian or Oriental?"

"She was white," he said.

Not Josie then. I opened my purse and took out the photos of the four women who'd been in the OR. "Would you mind taking a look at these and telling me if any of them resembles the woman he was with?"

Tom looked them over and shook his head.

"Definitely not. The woman was much younger and had very dark hair."

"You've been a major help, Tom. Thank you."

"So," I said, as Andrea and I waited for the valet to retrieve our car, "We've now eliminated every woman I thought was a good prospect for Wesley's mistress. Daniel won't be happy when I tell him what I've found out."

I got home from Spago at about two-thirty, and Jane, my neighbor and car pool partner, dropped Zoe off about half an hour later.

"Have a good time, sweetheart?" I asked.

Zoe grinned and showed me her loot-bag.

"Mommy, remember the book you read to me, about not talking to strangers?"

"The one with the bears," I said.

"Well, a stranger was talking to me at Alissa's party in the park, but I wouldn't talk to him."

"Good for you, honey. Was he one of your friends' fathers?"

"I dunno?"

"What did he say to you?"

Zoe was opening her loot-bag and checking out the candy collection.

"He said, did I want him to take me home in his car. I ran away from him and found Jane." She opened a Tootsie Roll.

My stomach lurched. "What did he look like, Zoe?"

She shrugged. "I don't remember."

"Did Jane's mom see him?"

Zoe shrugged.

"Well, I'm very proud of you," I said. "It's very important

never to talk to a stranger, and never, ever to get in a car with one. You did exactly the right thing."

I was trying hard not to let my agitation frighten her. Could it have been Eddie? Could he have found out where I lived, and that I had a daughter? But how could he have known where Zoe was going to be this afternoon?

I was letting my imagination run away with me. The guy was probably just your run-of-the-mill psychotic pedophile. I was going to have to tell Emilia about this, and warn her to watch Zoe like a hawk. I wondered if I should tell Daniel too. Although, Daniel had enough to worry about. And short of becoming Zoe's personal, full-time bodyguard, there wasn't much he could do about any of this.

CHAPTER TWENTY-SEVEN

DANIEL SPENT THE DAY PESTERING THE LABORATORY technicians, and trying to decide if he was dealing with a natural death, a suicide or a homicide. Josie Otero had been found lying on her sofa, peacefully dead. There was a teapot, and a flowered china cup with tea dregs, on the coffee table next to her. They had searched her apartment, which was immaculate. But there was no sign of forced entry or violence. The only drugs in the house were Tylenol and antacids. The kitchen was perfectly neat, with an empty dishwasher, and all cups and dishes put away in the china cupboard. The dishtowel was damp, as if someone may have rinsed and dried a dish recently.

Daniel had the teapot and cup sent to the laboratory for analysis, and had asked that a toxicology screen be run on Josie's body as quickly as possible. The forensic team had done the usual check for fingerprints, fibers and blood.

By late afternoon, he had an answer. Josie had died from an overdose of Ambien, a commonly prescribed sleeping pill. The drug had been present in the cup, but not the teapot. No empty drug container had been found anywhere in the apartment.

Daniel and Brenda called every pharmacy within a two-mile radius of Josie's home and West Beverly and found no record of a prescription. Josie's address book gave them the name of her personal physician, who denied ever having prescribed any sleeping pills for her.

The death was looking more like a murder than an accidental suicide. Daniel sent a patrolman to canvass the neighbors. Meanwhile, he was going to check the whereabouts of everyone connected to Wesley's murder. He was not a believer in coincidences, and when someone involved in a murder case died suddenly, it was beyond suspicious.

It was almost ten o'clock, and I was contemplating turning in for the night, when Daniel finally called.

"You sound exhausted," I said. "What did you find?"

"Josie died of an overdose of Ambien, in a cup of tea. I don't think it was a suicide."

"Was there a suicide note?" I asked.

"Nothing," he said. "We're questioning all the neighbors to see if anyone came to visit that evening. The coroner thinks she died somewhere between five and seven p.m."

"I take it you think someone else put the sleeping pills in her drink."

"I can't prove it yet," Daniel said. "But, yes. Maybe she knew something and someone felt she needed to be shut up."

"Or maybe she killed Wesley, and couldn't live with the guilt. Perhaps she stole some Ambien from the hospital," I said. "But wouldn't it make the tea taste bitter?"

"I thought of that," Daniel said. "It was pretty strong, black China tea. As far as stealing it goes, isn't Ambien a controlled drug?"

I nodded. Not that he could see me. "It's kept under lock and key. They don't keep it in the operating room suite because it isn't used for surgery. But if she killed herself because she murdered Wesley, wouldn't you expect her to write a confession? What about alibis? Where was everyone, Saturday afternoon?"

"Well, Erica Templeton was at home after the funeral, in full view of at least fifty people, including Ashley and Mort Levine. Helen Johnson was at a movie with her husband. Martha Wells was doing her grocery shopping at the Ralph's in her neighborhood. And Adrienne Venning says she was at home, nursing a bad cold."

"You have been busy," I said. "Did you check on Sara as well?"

"We haven't been able to reach Sara. No one's been home all day and her car is gone. I've got a patrolman parked across the street. He'll notify us as soon as she gets back, from wherever she is."

I shrugged. I didn't think Sara was a serious suspect. I told Daniel about my lunch at Spago. "I assume you know most of this already."

"Actually not," he said. "Unfortunately, my resources are limited and the Templeton murder isn't the only one we're dealing with. There was another big gang blow-up in Venice last night. The trail you followed, should have been taken care of days ago by someone in the department, but I haven't had anyone to spare."

"Does that mean I should continue being Nancy Drew?" I asked.

"I'd rather you didn't," he said. "If I'm right about Josie, then we have a multiple killer, who won't hesitate to kill again, to protect his or her identity. If you get too close, you may be next, and I'd never forgive myself if you got hurt."

I was touched. I didn't realize Daniel felt protective about me. I never used to worry much about being protected. I always figured I was savvy enough to take care of myself. After all, I was a tough lady. Beth's death had changed all that. It made me realize that anyone was vulnerable to the whims of a sociopathic killer, and that no one, and no place, was safe. All you could do was lower the odds.

I kept wondering why the hell I still lived in Los Angeles. The odds of getting killed here had been getting a lot higher lately. I had fantasies of moving to some picturesque place, like Carmel or Mendocino, and opening a small, unpretentious medical office. Having grown up in New York, I'd always considered any place with a population of less than eight million to be a rural backwater, but getting older was changing my point of view. My need for glitz and excitement had diminished to a dull roar, and the prospect of being able to take a night-time stroll, without looking over my shoulder, was increasingly appealing. It must be the onset of middle age.

I blew Daniel a kiss over the phone and told him I missed having him in bed with me.

He offered to bring over Chinese food for dinner tomorrow and I agreed.

I set my alarm, put Zoe to bed, took a quick, hot shower, brushed out my hair and slipped between cool cotton sheets. I was asleep before I could finish the plot of my erotic fantasy.

CHAPTER TWENTY-EIGHT

ON MONDAY MORNING, OPPORTUNITY KNOCKED AND I couldn't resist answering. One of my first trimester obstetrical patients came in, complaining of spotting. A quick look with the ultrasound confirmed that her pregnancy was no longer viable. The fetal heart had stopped beating, and what should have been a ten-week sized baby, had stopped growing several weeks ago.

After breaking the news to her as gently as I could, I offered her a D&C under local anesthesia in my office, to empty the uterus. It turned out that she wanted to be completely asleep, under a general anesthetic. As she had eaten breakfast, I had to wait at least eight hours for her stomach to be completely empty before I could operate. So, I asked my secretary to try to get a surgical time at West Beverly Hospital for about 5:00 p.m. I knew that the evening shift came on at three, and I was hoping that my OR team would consist of at least one or two of the individuals who had been there the night Wesley was murdered. This didn't fall under the category of amateur detecting. I was just doing my job.

Daniel's project for the morning was to stop by the personnel office at L.A. County hospital, to see if he could elicit any useful information about Martha Wells. The hospital itself was huge, and a maze to the uninitiated. He followed a yellow line on the floor, through several twists and turns, past patients lying on gurneys in the hallways, in various stages of dress and distress. Large, Hispanic families were seated on the floors, and harried residents in scrubs and dirty white coats were attempting to answer everyone's demands simultaneously, in broken Spanish. He felt grateful to have health insurance.

The entrance to the inner sanctum of the personnel office was guarded by a young receptionist who was typing with the tips of her two-inch-long hot pink nails and chewing a wad of gum, simultaneously.

"Can I help you?" she asked, ceasing momentarily to chew.

"I'm Detective Ross from LAPD. I'd like to see the personnel supervisor."

"Yes, sir." She pressed a few buttons on her touchtone phone and announced him.

A few minutes later, he was greeted by a pleasant, gray-haired woman, in a neat tweed suit. "I'm Miss Hoskins. Would you care to come back to my office?"

He followed her through a grid of cubbyholes to a small, dreary office at the back of the room.

She closed the door and motioned him to sit down. "How can I help you?"

"My office is involved in investigating a murder case. One of the most important witnesses is a former employee of your hospital. It's my job to check the background of all the witnesses, so I need to have a look at her file. Her name is Martha Wells. She worked as an operating room nurse here, up until ten years ago."

Miss Hoskins pursed her lips. "Ten years ago, is a long time. Her file would be in storage, I'm afraid. I can have it sent to you, provided you have the appropriate identification and authorization."

A careful woman. He was impressed.

"I'd appreciate that," he said, showing her his badge. He opened his briefcase and pulled out his copy of Martha's personnel file from West Beverly Hospital. "Perhaps you could tell me if either of the two nursing supervisors who wrote these letters of recommendation are still employed here."

He slid a sheet of paper with the two names in her direction.

She turned on the PC terminal at her desk and typed in the information.

"Janet Dillon, the Cardiac Surgery OR Supervisor, still works here." She glanced at her watch. "She should be in the house. I can have her paged and see if she has time to talk to you."

"Thank you." He waited while she phoned, tapping his fingers on the arm of the chair and hoping he could get this conversation over with, before traffic built up again.

"Mrs. Dillon will be right up. We have a small office next door that we use for interviewing applicants. You're welcome to use it."

"I appreciate your time and help," he said. He handed her one of his cards. "Please feel free to call the station, if you need to verify my identity any further."

The interview room had no windows and consisted of a county regulation table and two chairs. Janet Dillon turned out to be a tall, attractive black woman in her fifties. She shook his hand and slid gracefully into the opposite chair.

"Miss Hoskins told me you had a few questions for me," she said. "What can I do for you?"

"Do you remember an operating room nurse named Martha Wells? She left here about ten years ago."

"Of course, I remember Martha," she said. "She was one of the best scrub techs we had. I was sorry to lose her."

"Do you have any idea why she left County?" Daniel asked. "I couldn't help noticing, when I reviewed her personnel file at West Beverly Hospital, that she seems to have taken a pay cut and moved to a less interesting and prestigious job when she left here. I would imagine that running a recovery room, in a small community hospital, would be pretty boring after being on the cardiac surgery team here."

Janet smiled. "I imagine it was boring. Maybe that's why she took the job. Nurses get burned out quickly here. The stress level is very high."

"So, you think she quit in order to have a lower stress job?" he asked.

"It's been a long time," Janet said. "But that is what I remember. I believe there was some tragedy in her family. I'm not sure I knew what it was. Martha was a very private person. I do know that she left here shortly after."

"About ten years ago, did you know a Dr. Wesley Templeton? He would have been a fellow in plastic surgery at that time."

Janet shook her head. "The cardiac surgery service is pretty self-contained. Our nurses don't scrub in on anything but heart cases. I'd have had no reason to run into him."

"What about Martha Wells? Did she ever scrub in on the plastic surgery service?"

"Not to my knowledge."

Another dead end. He supposed Martha could have known Wesley, but he doubted that he'd have been involved in her family tragedy, whatever it was. He'd try to talk to her again anyway. Maybe she could tell him something helpful about Josie Otero.

CHAPTER TWENTY-NINE

B Y THE TIME HE RETRIEVED HIS CAR FROM THE parking lot and eased it onto the San Bernardino freeway, traffic had begun to converge on the downtown interchange. He slipped a classical Vivaldi CD into his player and let the music soothe him, as he crawled along at twenty miles an hour, and contemplated his next move. As always, he found driving through the eastern edge of downtown a depressing ride. It was run down, dirty and industrial, a dismal contrast to the gleaming skyscrapers clustered to the north. He glanced at his watch, trying to decide how long it would take to get back to the Westside, and took advantage of his Bluetooth to call Hannah in her office.

"Hi, beautiful," he said. "I was just thinking about you."

"You're probably hungry," she said. "Where are you?"

"I'm always hungry. It's genetic and has nothing to do with you. I'm in my car, just coming up on the Vermont Avenue off-ramp. I was just at the L.A. County Hospital, making inquiries about Martha Wells."

"Find out anything interesting?"

"Not so far. I thought I'd try to talk to her again, some-time this week".

"Does her alibi hold up for the time of Josie's death?" Hannah asked.

"Yeah, it does. The clerk at Ralph's knows her and checked her out at about six o'clock. Her neighbor saw her leave to go shopping at five, and helped her bring her groceries upstairs at six-fifteen. She lives about twenty minutes from the hospital and reported to work at West Beverly at seven p.m. It doesn't look as if she had time for tea. How do you feel about lemon chicken and shrimp with lobster sauce for dinner? I could bring us takeout."

"Sounds great," she said. "I've got to do a little emer-gency surgery after I'm done at the office, but it should be quick. I'll be home by seven. Don't forget noodles for Zoe."

The evening OR team consisted of an anesthesiologist I didn't know, a male scrub tech (who was apparently a replacement for Josie), and Helen Johnson. She was a very slow circulator, waddling gracelessly through the OR, as she collected the suction machine, the drapes, and the prep kit. She certainly didn't fit the image of the young woman who had dined with Wesley at Spago. Martha was also on duty, and helped Helen bring my patient in.

I finished my five-minute scrub and entered the OR to be gowned and gloved.

"I hear it's been a very bad week at West Beverly. I heard about Dr. Templeton," I said.

"Did you know him?" the anesthesiologist asked.

"Not well," I said. "He was in the class behind mine in medical school. Do the police have any clue who killed him?"

"Not that we've been told," Helen said. "And let me tell

you, it makes us all very nervous. None of us are going anywhere alone at night."

I couldn't blame her. I'd made a point of changing into my scrubs before I left the office. There was no way I was going into the ladies' locker room alone, after this case.

Helen and I positioned my patient. The anesthesiologist put in an oral airway and put her to sleep with a mask. The procedure would be rapid. I put in a speculum, dilated the cervix to 8 mm and suctioned out the remains of the pregnancy. The whole process took less than ten minutes.

"Thanks everyone," I said. "That was very efficient."

The anesthesiologist woke her up and we transferred her to a gurney. Helen wheeled her into recovery and left her in Martha's hands. While Martha was taking her first set of vital signs, I dictated the operative note and started writing orders.

"You must all be feeling very stressed," I said to Martha. "I heard about Dr. Templeton and Josie. What a tragedy. You look worn out."

"I guess I feel worn down, by having too many people I know die in too short a time span," she replied.

"It was a shame about Josie," I said. "I only met her once, but she seemed like a sweet young woman."

Martha nodded. "Rumor mill says she killed herself. That true?"

"I don't know any more than you do. Any idea why she would have done something like that? Was she depressed?"

"Not depressed," Martha said. "More like jumpy. I think Dr. Templeton's murder really upset her. Come to think of it, she did ask me last week if I remembered the name of that police detective who questioned us. I got the impression she wanted to talk to him."

"Did you tell her his name?" I asked.

She shook her head. "I couldn't remember it, either. I suggested she ask someone in administration. They probably wrote it down somewhere."

"You have any idea why she wanted to talk to him?" I asked.

"I'm sorry, I don't." She looked up at me, distress mirrored in her kindly face. "You don't think Josie could possibly have killed Dr. Templeton and then herself, do you?"

Not an unreasonable conclusion, unless you knew that Josie had been murdered.

"I doubt it," I said, hoping I sounded reassuring. "She certainly didn't strike me as a killer."

Martha buried her face in her hands. "So much violence in this city," she whispered.

I could see tears forming in the corners of her eyes.

"You know my boy was killed, ten years ago. He was only eight. He was playing in the schoolyard. They had a day care program for working parents. Some gang boys drove by and shot a few kids just for sport. They never caught them."

I reached across the table and touched her arm gently. "I didn't know. I'm so sorry."

I had a sudden horrible vision of Zoe, a bullet wound in her forehead, lying still on the ground.

"That's when I moved my family from Watts to Culver City and started working nights. That way, I could drive my girl home from school every day, and keep her off the street in the afternoon. She's in college now." Martha looked up at me and smiled.

"She's lucky to have you for a mother," I said.

I closed the chart and handed it to her, as I left recovery.

CHAPTER THIRTY

I MADE IT HOME, TOOK OFF MY SCRUBS AND PUT ON some shorts and a T-shirt. Then I greeted my daughter with a hug that lasted much longer than usual.

Daniel arrived about five minutes later and gave me a lingering kiss and two warm brown bags.

I finished setting the table, put the food out, and dished up a bowl of noodles for Zoe, who wanted to eat them in front of the television set. It was a practice I normally discouraged, unless the dinner table conversation was likely to be a topic unsuitable for children. Given what was on both of our minds, an *Octonauts* marathon seemed like a good idea for Zoe.

Daniel picked up his chopsticks, speared a piece of lemon chicken and followed it down with a gulp of iced tea. "So," he said. "How did your surgery go?"

"Fine," I said. "I did the case at West Beverly. Helen Johnson was my scrub tech and Martha Wells was in the recovery room. Everyone is very spooked about the murder and Josie's supposed suicide. I understand, by the way, why you didn't think Helen was a candidate for Wesley's mistress."

Daniel almost choked on a piece of shrimp and took another sip of tea.

"I had a chance to chat with Martha after the case. She was in tears over Josie. I found out that her son was killed in a random gang shooting ten years ago, when he was eight. That's why she left County and took an evening job. More important, she told me that Josie had been very jumpy all week, and had wanted to talk to you. She couldn't remember your name and asked Martha for it. Martha didn't remember either, but suggested Josie check with administration."

Daniel took a deep breath, and reached over the table for my free hand. "Look, Hannah, this is starting to make me uncomfortable. You're a great doctor, but you're not a police detective. You aren't trained to protect yourself, in case of violence. You're going after a person who's killed twice, and who will probably kill again if threatened. I appreciate all the help you've given me so far, but I want you to stop."

"You want me to stop, because you're afraid I'll get hurt? Or because you're afraid I might succeed?"

"If you think my ego is so inadequate, that it can't tolerate you solving one of my cases, maybe you need a new boyfriend."

I stuffed several shrimp into my mouth and chewed vigorously, trying to control my temper. I wondered if he had any idea that he was treating me like a five year old.

"Give me some credit for a little intelligence," I said. "I'm not going to meet any of your suspects in a back alley somewhere, and I'm not drinking any home-brewed tea. I was just doing my job, in a hospital where I have staff privileges.

I figured it wouldn't hurt if I was able to pick up a little information on the side."

Daniel glared at her. "And I want you to stop, because I love you and I don't want you dead."

"And I want to help you solve this case, so that Sara gets crossed off the suspect list. Which reminds me, where is Sara?"

"According to the guy I have watching her apartment, she arrived home about an hour ago, brought a suitcase up from her car, and immediately went out again. She was obviously out of town somewhere. I imagine I'll be able to reach her later in the evening."

Daniel got up, took his plate into the kitchen, and stuck it in the dishwasher.

I could tell he was pissed and I decided I needed to defuse him. I wasn't really up for a fight. Besides, I knew he was angry only because he worried about me.

"How about some ice cream?" I asked.

Daniel shook his head and sat back down at the table.

I got up, stood behind him, and began kneading the tension out of his neck and back.

"By the way," I said, "I almost forgot to tell you, I have a new unlisted number. I was getting a few too many heavy-breathers."

Daniel turned toward me, suddenly alert. "How long has this been going on?"

"Not long, but the guy's persistent. His name's Eddie and he's taken to phoning me at four in the morning. It's making me antsy."

"Why the hell didn't you tell me about this before?" Daniel's eyes were like steel.

"I didn't want to bother you. You've had enough to do."

"You're meddling in the middle of two murder cases,

you're getting threatening phone calls, and you don't even bother to mention it. What were you waiting for, someone to kill you? Or try to kidnap Zoe?"

My heart skipped a beat as I remembered what Zoe had said about the man in the park. "I've been taking care of myself and of Zoe for a hell of a long time before you walked into my life. I am not a helpless little female who needs a big strong policeman to protect her. I'm sorry if I offended you."

"So, you think *I* have a problem, just because I don't want you to wind up on a slab in the mortuary, like Beth?"

"Leave Beth out of this."

"I can't leave her out of this. I'm the guy who washed her blood off the floor for you, so you could go into her bedroom without throwing up. Or have you forgotten?"

I shook my head. "I haven't forgotten. I know you care about me, but you obviously don't respect my intelligence enough to realize that I won't take any unnecessary risks."

"And you don't respect the fact that I do this for a living, and I've got a very keen instinct about what's safe and what's dangerous."

"What's dangerous?" I asked.

"Staying here any longer is dangerous. If I stay one more minute, we're both going to wind up saying some things we may not be able to take back in the morning."

I wasn't so sure we hadn't done that already. I locked the door after him, stuck the rest of the plates in the dishwasher, and called the recovery room at West Beverly Hospital to check on my patient.

There was no way in hell I was dropping this. I made myself a mental note to call Sara tomorrow.

Daniel slid into the driver's seat of his car and took a deep breath. It wasn't like him to get so angry. Hannah had to be the most stubborn woman he'd ever met. While he had to admit that her help and her insight had always been invaluable, she had no clue about the potential danger her amateur detective antics could cause. This wasn't an Agatha Christie mystery and she wasn't Miss Marple. If he wasn't so crazy about her, he'd have shut her out of the loop completely, to protect her. But he knew that wouldn't work. She'd plunge ahead anyway and potentially get herself into trouble. He was better off walking a fine line, and keeping a leash on her investigative efforts.

When I reached my office the next morning, there were three phone messages on my desk. They all said to call Detective Ross, ASAP. I figured he wanted to apologize.

"Daniel, it's me. What is it?" I said.

"Bad news." His voice didn't sound at all apologetic. "I wanted to talk to Sara last night, but she never returned to her apartment. I found out why this morning. She was the victim of a hit-and-run. She's in the intensive care unit at L.A. Memorial."

CHAPTER THIRTY-ONE

THE LOS ANGELES MEMORIAL SURGICAL INTENSIVE care unit was on the seventh floor. There was a telephone just outside the door, and a sign said that visitors were admitted only for five minutes out of every hour and which requested them to announce their presence. I ignored it and headed inside to the nursing desk, wearing my white coat and my hospital ID.

"I'm Dr. Kline. I'm here to see Sara Hellman."

"She's in room six, doctor. Do you need the chart?" asked the ward clerk.

I was a little perturbed by this breech of security. Because of Sara's connection to Wesley, the police were treating this hit-and-run as an attempted homicide until proven otherwise. They'd assigned a police guard just to be certain the killer didn't stop by to finish the job. I wasn't Sara's doctor, and I wasn't a consultant on her case. I was also not well known to the secretary, as my patients rarely required intensive care, and I spent little time in the Surgical ICU. Clearly, anyone with a white coat and an appropriate title could get in to see her.

"May I help you, sir?"

The clerk turned to Daniel, who had followed me inside.

He presented his ID. "I'm Detective Ross with the LAPD. You can okay me with the guard over there. I'm with the doctor."

I could tell that Daniel was still in a lousy mood. He didn't smile and he barely acknowledged my presence. His voice was all cop.

By this time, the guard had noticed us and nodded to Daniel. We crossed the unit to Sara's door.

The surgical intensive care unit was a large, bright room, crowded with medical personnel and electronic equipment. A central station contained charts, several secretaries and a row of monitors, which gave continuous readouts of EKG's and laboratory data. The patient rooms were arrayed around the periphery, each with large glass windows, which enabled the nurses to keep a constant eye on their charges, even when they were not with them. On the wall next to each door was a built-in computer screen, which allowed the nurses to update patient information.

I paused at the door and glanced at Sara's latest data.

"I'm Angie, Miss Hellman's nurse," said a young blonde woman, smiling at me. "I've got her chart for you, doctor."

"Thank you."

"I'm afraid she won't be able to talk to you," Angie said. "She's still unconscious."

"What does neurology think? Have they seen her yet?"

"The neurologist who saw her this morning is optimistic," Angie said. "There's a skull fracture, some cerebral edema and concussion, but no evidence of anoxia or hemorrhage. We're treating her with steroids. Hopefully, she'll regain consciousness in a few days, but she's going to have a rough time. Multiple fractures, a ruptured spleen and a pneumothorax."

"Would you mind translating all that into English for me?" Daniel asked.

The news was bad, but it could have been a lot worse. This was one of these situations where you just had to wait it out and hope for the best.

"Sometimes, I forget that not everyone speaks the language," I said. "It means that Sara has some swelling of the brain tissue because of the blow that fractured the skull, but it doesn't seem as if the brain was deprived of oxygen, so there shouldn't be any permanent damage once she recovers. She's had her spleen removed, and one of her lungs collapsed because of a fractured rib."

"I'm so sorry," Daniel said. "Are you okay? It must be hard for you, seeing a friend this way."

I nodded. I was afraid that if I said anything I might start to cry.

Daniel refrained from reminding me that this is the sort of thing that can happen to amateurs who mess with murder investigations.

I appreciated his restraint.

The young policeman, stationed by the door, opened the room and I got my first good look at Sara. Sara's eyes were closed, her face white and pasty. A tangle of dark hair, with sweat soaked roots, was splayed out over the pillow. A white plastic tube, attached to a respirator, protruded from her mouth. A plastic bag at the foot of the bed contained urine, and two others at the side of the bed were filled with bloody fluid. IV's dripped into both arms and one leg was wrapped in a large cast and elevated.

"She has a drain from her abdomen where they removed the spleen," Angie explained to Daniel. "And that's the chest tube. As the lung heals and regains its ability to expand, the drainage will decrease and we won't need it anymore."

I took it all in and walked closer, to touch Sara's hand. It was clammy and curled up like an infant's. A drop of spittle escaped from the side of her mouth and dripped toward her neck. Angie dabbed at it with a towel and suctioned her mouth and throat efficiently, with a long plastic catheter.

I wanted to kill the bastard who'd done this to her. Poor Sara, life just kept dealing her one blow after another, and every time she managed to crawl back up onto her feet, something else happened. I wondered if this was just a horrible coincidence, or if it was really the work of the same person who'd killed Wesley.

"You're going to be okay, Sara," I whispered, stroking her hair gently. They say people can hear you, even if they're unconscious. "You're safe in the hospital. It's going to be okay."

I turned and saw Daniel standing at the door, watching me. His face looked a little pasty.

"Angie, this is Lieutenant Ross," I said. "He's investigating Miss Hellman's accident."

Angie smiled at Daniel and he motioned for us to talk outside.

"Any news?" I asked, closing the ICU door behind me.

Daniel shook his head. "I picked up Sara's purse from nursing administration. It's got her house keys in it, but nothing else of much interest. I thought perhaps her apartment might give us a clue as to where she was last night. Would you like to come with me? You know her so much better than I do, you might notice something I'd totally overlook."

It sounded like a peace offering of sorts so I accepted.

Daniel didn't much feel like making conversation as they

drove out of the parking lot. ICU's were unnerving; all those drains and respirators made him feel queasy. He was impressed at the way Hannah took it all in stride. Then again, he'd managed to get used to the sight of homicide victims. Maybe it was all a question of what constituted a day's work.

He hoped he wasn't making a mistake taking Hannah with him. It was certainly against regulations, but he'd rather keep a close eye on her, than wonder if she was taking off on her own, to do something he would consider risky. Maybe allowing her to help, under tightly-controlled conditions, was his best bet for avoiding an argument and keeping her safe.

CHAPTER THIRTY-TWO

S ARA'S CONDOMINIUM HAD THAT MUSTY SMELL A place gets when it's locked up tight for a while. Daniel flipped on the lights, and I opened a window to let in some fresh air. The downstairs was immaculate, every accessory in place and barely a sign that a real person lived here. I kept hoping for a dirty sock on the carpet or a half-empty cup of coffee in the sink. I was always uncomfortable with Sara's obsessive neatness. The place reminded me of a model home, ready for a real estate agent to show off to a client. The living room, dining room and powder room revealed nothing promising. We headed upstairs.

The master bedroom was spacious and airy, with a balcony and skylights, which allowed streaks of sunlight to tiptoe across the pale peach carpet. Sara and Wesley's old king-sized bed took up most of the room, two pillows on one side and none on the other. Sara's suitcase was sitting open, but still packed, on the bed. Daniel and I went through it: a few summer dresses, shoes and stockings, underwear, a nightgown, toiletries and a novel.

What was of interest was the envelope lying on the

bedside table, which contained her baggage claim check, a carbon copy of a contract with Avis, and the itinerary from her travel agent for a round trip to Hartford, Connecticut.

"What in the world was she doing in Hartford?" Daniel asked. "Did she know anyone there?"

"I have no idea," I said. "We may need to wait until she regains consciousness to ask her."

"If she ever does," Daniel said.

"Don't say that. You think the same person did it, don't you?"

He nodded. "It's too much of a coincidence, to be a coincidence. I think Sara got close to something she wasn't supposed to touch and someone tried to kill her. Maybe this will convince you that playing Miss Marple isn't a lark."

"I never thought it was."

"Did it ever occur to you, that you could be next on the killer's list of nosy people who know too much?"

"I guess it hadn't. Obviously, it's occurred to you." I turned away from him.

"Why don't I check her dresser? You can see if there's anything in the study," he said.

The study looked like the room in which Sara spent most of her time. The walls were lined with floor-to-ceiling shelves full of books. There was a TV, a DVD player, a comfortable sofa upholstered in beige-colored velvet, and an antique fruitwood coffee table with a full ashtray. A lingering scent of smoke made me cough. I opened the sliding doors to the balcony, to let in some air, and turned my attention to Sara's desk. It was full of papers, organized into neat manila folders. A directory of the American Medical Association was lying near the telephone.

I examined the folders carefully. The first one contained bills to be paid. The second had an assortment of health insurance brochures. The third one had legal documents relating to Sara's latest effort to bring Wesley to court. It looked as if they'd been arguing over the pension plan. The last one contained letters.

There were about a dozen of them, written over a period of about a year, and addressed to Wesley at a Cambridge post office box. There were no return addresses on the envelopes, but the creamy, embossed stationary was monogrammed with the name Ellie Bennett.

January 26

My Darling Wesley,

I keep thinking about our last night together, and wishing that fate had thrown you in my path before I married Gordon. The move has been difficult for me. I'm not used to the life of a suburban Connecticut housewife and Gordon has been spending all his time promoting his new practice. I feel lonely, tired, and find myself continually daydreaming about us. I shall try to find an excuse for a trip to Boston soon.

My love always,
Ellie

∽

April 11

Darling,

I felt the baby move for the first time today. What a miracle. I can't wait for it to be born, so I can have a part of you with me always. Your letters warm me and make me happy. There is something about pregnancy that creates a state of complete tranquility for me. I can think about how impossible this situation is with the intellectual part of my brain and cut off its emotional impact. I'm busy decorating the nursery and fantasizing about names. What do you think of William for a boy and Valerie for a girl?

I love you,

El

October 1

Wesley, my love,

Your daughter, Valerie Elise Bennett, was born Saturday night at seven-thirty, after a short and uneventful labor. How I wish you could have been with me. She is so lovely. She has your dark hair and your wonderful eyes. I can't wait to show her to you. I don't think Gordon suspects, although he did make a comment about recessive genes when he saw her blue eyes. I can't believe it's really happened—our child—our beautiful Valerie.

January 18

Dear Wesley,

I can't stop thinking about seeing you last week, and my joy at being able to show you your daughter. Yet, I also haven't slept for days, thinking about the things you said. You're right that Valerie's welfare has to take precedence over our own needs and feelings. Since we've decided we can't hurt Gordon by breaking up my marriage to be together then—painful as it is—I agree that we should probably stop seeing one another. I understand how horrible it would be for you to keep seeing your daughter without being able to claim her, and I'm deeply touched by the sacrifice you are making in leaving her life now, before you find it impossible.

Just know how much I love you and how grateful I am for your incredible gift of Valerie.

"And she believed that bullshit!" said a note in the margin in Sara's handwriting.

So, these were the letters Sara had discovered in the safe deposit box. She hadn't mentioned, during our dinner, that Ellie Bennett lived in Connecticut. Could Sara have flown to Hartford to find her? I turned to the AMA directory and noticed there was a scrap of paper marking Sara's place. The page was in the B section and eight Bennetts were listed. Gordon Bennett M.D. was an orthopedic surgeon in Darby, Connecticut.

"I've got it," I called out to Daniel, who was still searching through Sara's drawers.

CHAPTER THIRTY-THREE

"SHE WAS GOING TO CONNECTICUT TO FIND Wesley's old mistress and his daughter."

Daniel shook his head. "Why would she have wanted to do that?"

"Unfinished business," I said. "I understand it perfectly. She woke up one morning and discovered her whole life was a lie. She needed to sort everything out and discover what was real and what wasn't. What's even more interesting, is that this woman apparently lives in Darby, Connecticut. Didn't you tell me that Adrienne Venning had practiced there?"

Daniel shrugged. "I talked to Adrienne's husband a few days ago. He answered all my questions, just like a lawyer, but the bottom line was that he met and married her in L.A. a year ago and corroborated everything she told us. If he's telling the truth, she couldn't have murdered Josie Otero. But she has no alibi for Wesley."

"And Sara's accident?"

"I don't know yet. I thought, instead of asking people for

alibis, I'd have some of my guys take a look at the cars of everyone connected with the case. Maybe we'll get lucky."

"Great," I said. "So, when are we leaving for Hartford?"

"We? The LAPD doesn't have that kind of a budget. I'll have to call the Darby police and have them question Mrs. Bennett."

"I have a better idea," I said. "My in-laws live in Hartford, and Zoe hasn't seen her cousins since Beth's funeral. Why don't I take a four-day weekend and stop in Darby, while I'm visiting. I have a feeling that the answer's there. I think it would be a mistake to miss it, by getting our information third hand."

"Believe it or not, I actually think that's a good idea." Daniel said. "It will get you both out of the reach of whoever's doing all this—at least, for the weekend."

I went back to the office, to let them know I'd be out of town for a few days, and to see how many patients I'd need to reschedule to make it possible. Fortunately, no one was due to deliver for at least two weeks, I didn't have any surgery booked for Monday, and Ruth was on call this weekend. When I told her I had some family stuff I needed to deal with, she said she didn't mind covering Friday and Monday. I promised to reciprocate the following week.

I was feeling much more mellow by the time I got home, but Emilia's news completely ruined my mood.

"He call again, Hannah, Eddie. He get the new phone number."

"He what?"

I'd barely memorized the new number myself and I hadn't had a chance to give it to any but critical professional contacts. This was getting scary. I was being stalked by someone with connections I didn't understand, but they were obviously good enough to get him an unlisted number.

"You tell Daniel?" Emilia asked. "He catch that Eddie."

"I'll let him know. Before I leave for Hartford, I'll arrange with the phone company to have all my phone calls traced. If this guy calls again while I'm gone Emilia, you call Daniel."

It was least I could do. He'd have a fit if I didn't tell him, and I owed him one for taking me to Sara's apartment. Emilia didn't look too happy but she said nothing. I went to my bedroom and started packing.

Daniel was not happy when Hannah called that evening to tell him about Eddie and the new unlisted number.

"How many people have your new number?" he asked.

"Not many. You, Ruth, my office, the exchange, and Labor and Delivery. None of those people would ever give out my home number."

"I need you to document every phone call you can remember, and file a police report before you leave tomorrow. I'll fax you the form and you can just fax it back to me."

"Is that really necessary?"

Daniel sighed. "If you want the phone company to enable call tracing on your phone, they will only provide the information to the police, and it needs to link to a police report. The sooner you do this, the sooner we can catch this guy."

"Do you think this is connected to Wesley's murder?"

"I don't know," Daniel said, "but I'm not taking any chances."

He told her that she, or Emilia, needed to dial *57 if Eddie called. He would receive the number and take it from there. But it made him doubly glad that Hannah and Zoe would be gone for four days. He didn't think Hannah could get into trouble interviewing an orthopedic surgeon. In the meantime, he'd see if he could solve this problem.

Compared to a murder investigation, it should be a piece of cake. And he knew he could count on Emilia to let him know if there were any more calls.

CHAPTER THIRTY-FOUR

Ben's parents, Irving and Evelyn Kline, still lived in the modest mansion I had seen for the first time, almost twenty years ago, during Christmas vacation from Harvard. Compared to my folks' two-bedroom apartment in Flatbush, their house had appeared awesomely rich. From the outside, at least, it still exuded an air of opulence, velvet green front lawn, sparkling brass fixtures and an English garden in full bloom.

Irving had the front door open, before I turned off the engine on my Hertz rent-a-car.

"Where's my favorite grandchild?" He was beaming as we walked up the driveway, suitcase in hand.

Zoe broke into a run, as he held out his arms for a hug. "Hi, Grandpa. Thank you for my Barbie doll. It was my best birthday present ever."

Actually, Zoe never played with Barbie dolls. She had at least five of them, but she was a polite little girl and I'd reminded her to say thank you. Grandpa had sent the doll along with a five-figure contribution to her college fund.

I kissed Irving on the cheek, and refused to let him take

my luggage, as he ushered us into the front hall. The house was dim in the late afternoon and unnaturally quiet. All my memories of it included noise: classical music playing in the living room; Cora, the housekeeper, fussing and bustling; Ben's twin brothers, Michael and Mitch, arguing or watching loud television. The twins were now in their thirties, married, and the fathers of Zoe's cousins. They'd taken over Irving's highly successful insurance agency. Cora had passed on a few years ago, and been replaced by a series of live-in nurses for the failing Evelyn. I glanced in the living room as we crossed the hall to the stairs. Still elegant and comfortable, but fading. There was a fine sheen of dust on the hall table. The familiar smell of lemon polish was absent.

"How's Mother?" I asked Irving. I'd never felt comfortable calling Evelyn, "Mother," but she'd expressed a strong preference for the title, after Ben and I were married.

Irving shook his head. "Not good. She's still in the wheelchair, and she has no appetite and no interest in anything. I can't get her to leave the house."

"Maybe Zoe will cheer her up," I said.

Zoe was on her way up the stairs to the guest rooms. Irving and I followed.

"That's not the worst part." His eyes started to tear. "Her mind is going. Sometimes, I think she doesn't even know who I am. I haven't been able to leave her alone for months."

"Irving, why didn't you tell me?"

He shrugged. "You've had your own problems. What could you have done about it?"

I squeezed his hand.

Zoe was at the top of the stairs, waiting for us. "Which way, Mommy?"

I glanced at Irving.

"I've put you both in the twins' old room. I hope that's okay," he said.

"Perfect." I was touched by his sensitivity.

The other choices had been Ben's old room, or Beth's, or the guest room where Ben and I had always stayed after we were married. The twins' room had two neatly-made single beds, some banners from the University of Connecticut, and a few old athletic trophies. Michael had been on the college swim team. Mitch had gone out for track. The room felt empty and impersonal.

"Evelyn is in our room," Irving said. "Come, when you're ready."

I opened my suitcase, hung a few things on hangers, and waited for Zoe to go to the bathroom. Then, I splashed some water on my face, freshened my lipstick, and headed down the hall.

"Hello, Mother," I said. "I've brought Zoe to see you."

Evelyn was seated in a large armchair by the window, her lap covered with a baby blue Afghan, her wheelchair within easy reach. Her shoulder-length gray hair hung lank around her shriveled face. She was wearing a cream silk robe with rose piping, a pair of fuzzy pink bedroom slippers, and pearl earrings. Her face had been made up with powder, rouge, and bright pink lipstick that strayed outside the outline of her lips. I kissed her cheek and smelt Arpege by Lanvin.

"Hello, dear." She gave me a bright smile. "Zoe, come give Grandma a kiss."

Zoe looked a little intimidated. I suspect she couldn't remember the last time she'd seen her grandmother, and didn't much take to kissing strangers. I gave her a little shove and she approached the chair, and accepted Evelyn's embrace.

"I bet you'd like some milk and cookies," Evelyn said. "I'll ring for Cora."

She reached for a silver bell on the side table and shook it vigorously.

"I hope you brought Ben with you," she continued, turning her attention to me. "I know how busy he is, but the least he could do is come see his sick mother."

"I'm sorry, Mother," I said. "Ben couldn't come this visit."

Her face fell. "His work must be so important. We hardly ever see him, but he writes such nice letters. Irving reads them to me."

"He sent his love," I said, trying to keep my voice steady.

Zoe was looking at us as if we'd both gone bonkers. She was about to say something, when Irving came in, followed by a young woman in a nurse's uniform, wheeling a teacart. There was a plate of butter cookies, a glass of milk and an assortment of herb teas.

"Thank you, Cora," Evelyn said.

The woman nodded.

"This is Bernice," Irving said, introducing her to me in a low voice. "Evelyn likes to call all her nurses, Cora."

"I see."

"So, how is that daughter of mine?" Evelyn asked. "I hope you're doing something to get her married again, before it's too late for us to have another grandchild. Beth never did have any sense when it came to men."

Irving gave me an imploring look.

"I'll do my best, Mother." I said. "Excuse me for just a few minutes. I want to get Zoe something to play with while we talk. We'll be right back."

I took Zoe's hand, and her glass of milk, and pulled her out of the room before she could say anything.

"Mommy, I don't understand. I thought Aunt Beth was dead. Is Ben the same as Daddy?"

I sat down on the bed and pulled her onto my lap.

"Do you remember when Aunt Beth died, I told you that we never completely lose the people we love? They're always there in our memory."

"I remember," Zoe said.

"Well, Aunt Beth and Ben, your father, are alive in Grandma's imagination. Sometimes, when people get very old, they can't tell the difference between what's real and what's imaginary. It would make Grandma very sad right now, if we reminded her that Beth and Daddy aren't really alive."

"Okay, Mommy. We'll play pretend."

"Thanks, honey, I knew you'd understand."

We found a puzzle for Zoe and headed back to Evelyn's room.

Irving met us halfway there and motioned us downstairs. "She's sleeping. Too much excitement."

I nodded. "She said you've been reading her Ben's letters."

"His old ones, from Harvard. He used to write every week. I have a whole carton of them."

We went downstairs, listened to some music for a while, and then I made us all soup and tuna sandwiches for dinner. I let Zoe stay up until ten, then tucked her into Michael's bed.

I wasn't tired, just drained and too antsy to attempt to sleep, with my body on L.A. time. I tiptoed into Ben's old room and turned on the light. It was pretty much as I remembered it: twin bed, plaid spread, early American desk, empty except for a green blotter framed in dark leather. The wooden bookshelves held a few old high school texts; the walls, an old Yale banner and some class photos. I spotted Ben in the next-to-the-last row, smiling and squinting into the camera.

Beth's room was next door. That was harder. I'd first seen it when she was actually living here, a room cluttered with the paraphernalia of a bright high school student. Most of the personal items had been moved to California. I'd sorted through them and disposed of them after her death. The bed was still covered with the old yellow spread, with its pattern of baby ducklings. A white, wicker rocking chair still stood in the corner. The bookshelves and the desktop were empty.

I closed the door and headed back downstairs, to make myself a cup of hot chocolate. I hadn't realized how hard it would be for me to come back here. Evelyn wasn't so badly off after all. She was managing to cope in the least painful way possible. A large part of me envied her delusions.

CHAPTER THIRTY-FIVE

EMILIA WAS A PISTOL, DANIEL THOUGHT, AFTER SHE had dialed *57 and phoned him. Hannah was so lucky to have such a loyal employee. It hadn't taken long for Eddie to resurface. He phoned at nine in the evening, and Emilia, who had stayed over to intercept any calls, answered.

"She not here and she no want to talk to you. Why you keep calling?"

Daniel got the number from the phone company. It was an extension at Memorial Hospital. He called the chief of hospital security and explained that someone had been using their phones and harassing one of their staff physicians. The security chief was appropriately outraged and suggested that Daniel come on over. By the time Daniel arrived, the extension had been identified as a wall phone in a locker room in the basement, used by the male janitorial staff. Its access was by restricted key card.

Daniel had brought a fingerprint kit with him and obtained multiple excellent prints. The list of employees working that night with access included only one with the name Edward. He was assigned to the floor that included

Labor and Delivery. The men went upstairs and interviewed the ward clerk. Labor and Deliver was low-tech. They kept their physician contact information in a black, three-ring binder on the front desk. Each physician had a page with office, home, cell, exchange and back-line phone numbers. Hannah's had recently been updated. Daniel took some fingerprints off the plastic covering her page.

By the end of the shift, Eddie was in custody and Daniel was feeling very self-satisfied.

He couldn't wait to begin the interrogation, and to see Hannah's face when he broke the news.

Before leaving L.A., I'd phoned Dr. Bennett's office in Darby, and made an appointment to see him. I said I was a physician from Los Angeles and wanted to consult him on a case. His receptionist penciled me in for fifteen minutes at eleven o'clock, plenty of time to see him, return to Hartford and make our late afternoon flight home.

Darby was about an hour southeast of Hartford, a lush suburban community right on Long Island Sound. The downtown, if you could call it that, was a cutesy street that ran along the water, with lots of Cape Cod-style boutiques and family stores. Darby Community Hospital was a little inland, at the crest of a gentle hill that had a view of the water. A small, low-rise medical building, across from the hospital, boasted the offices of two orthopedic surgeons, a family practice group, and a gynecologist.

The waiting room was tastefully appointed in hunter green, with a long sofa, two wing chairs and a wall full of artfully arranged British hunting lithographs. I registered with the receptionist, settled myself in one of the wing chairs, and alternated my attention between the horses and hounds on the walls and the cartoons in The New Yorker. Dr. Bennett, being a typical physician, was forty-five minutes late.

I thought hard about how to approach him. The crux of the problem was that I didn't know if he knew that Valerie was some other man's daughter. If Ellie had kept it a secret all these years, I could destroy three people's lives by a thoughtless comment. I wondered if Sara had had similar scruples, or if she was so hurt and so bent on revenge, that she didn't care.

At eleven forty-five, I was ushered into Dr. Bennett's consultation room. He was sitting behind a large rosewood desk, in a black leather chair. A silver-framed photo, next to his telephone, showed a slim blonde woman and two small boys at the beach. He stood up, shook my hand, and motioned me to be seated in the leather and chrome chair opposite his. Attractive. Mid-forties, gray hair slicked back, thinning at the temples. Thin and wiry, he had a serious face with bushy eyebrows and a slightly receding chin. Nice smile. He was dressed in neatly pressed blue scrubs, and a white coat with his name embroidered on the breast pocket: Gordon Bennett, Orthopedics.

"I understand you want to consult me on a case, Dr. Kline," he said. "It must be pretty important to bring you all the way from Los Angeles. How can I help you?"

"A patient of mine, who is a witness in a major medical malpractice case, was the victim of a hit-and-run driver a week ago. She was badly injured. In fact, she's still unconscious. The police are investigating the possibility that it wasn't an accident. We know that she had been to see you the day before she was hit. Her name is Sara Hellman. The police are tracing all of Sara's movements prior to the accident. The detective on the case asked me to talk to you, since I was going to be in Connecticut on other business."

He nodded. "Sara Hellman did come to see me. She said she was an old college friend of my wife's from Boston. She claimed to have lost our home address and phone number, and wanted to get in touch. I told her she must be mistaken because Anne, my wife, went to school at the University of Michigan."

"Your wife isn't Ellie Bennett?" I asked.

"That's exactly what she said. Is Ellie involved in this malpractice case? She was my former wife, but we've been divorced for over twelve years. She left Connecticut and remarried quite a while ago."

"What about your daughter, Valerie? Is she living with her mother?"

A flicker of tension in his eyes, a tightening about his lips, or was I imagining it? "Valerie's a grown-up. She's on her own now."

"Were you able to put Sara in touch with your former wife?"

Dr. Bennett shook his head and toyed with an expensive-looking fountain pen. "Frankly, I don't keep in touch with Ellie any longer. We haven't had any contact since I sent her my last alimony and child support payment, on Valerie's eighteenth birthday. Anyway, I had no idea if that woman was telling me the truth. She may have been a creditor, or someone else Ellie didn't want to see. I had no reason to give her any information."

"Is that what you told her?"

"Essentially. I was polite about it. I just said that I didn't know where Ellie was living."

"What did she say?"

"She asked for Valerie's address. I refused."

"Then what?"

"She left. I didn't hear from her again."

"Dr. Bennett," I said. "It's possible that your former wife might be able to help us with some pertinent information. I need her married name and last known address." I handed him my identification and one of Daniel's cards. "Please feel free to verify my identity with the police detective in charge of the case."

"You want to tell me what the case is and what her connection might be?"

I shook my head. "I'm sorry. It's confidential."

"And if I refuse to give you the information?"

"Then the Los Angeles Police Department may have to arrange a search warrant with the local police."

"I see." He reached for a prescription pad and scribbled an address.

I glanced at it and slipped it into my purse.

"Anything else?" he asked. "I do have patients waiting."

"Just one more question. Do you happen to know a Dr. Adrienne Venning? She used to be an anesthesiologist here."

"Of course, I know Adrienne. Nice girl. Good doctor."

"Happen to know why she left Darby Community Hospital?" I asked.

He shrugged. "It's no secret. The whole hospital knew about it. She had some bad luck."

"What kind of bad luck?"

"A patient arrested and died on the operating table, just after Adrienne put her to sleep. It turned out the woman had had an undiagnosed cardiac problem. It wasn't Adrienne's fault, but the patient was the wife of one of the members of the hospital's board of trustees. Things got uncomfortable for her."

He looked at his watch.

I rose. "Thank you for your time, Dr. Bennett. I appreciate it."

He nodded. No smile.

I went out to the parking lot, slid into my seat and pulled the scrap of paper out of my purse. I wondered if Sara had managed to trace the former Mrs. Bennett, and if there was any link here to what had happened to her when she arrived home.

CHAPTER THIRTY-SIX

My flight from Hartford landed at LAX at eleven-thirty p.m., and I emerged into the fluorescent glare of the waiting room, carrying my purse on one shoulder and a sleeping, fifty-pound child on the other. I was trying to develop the optimal strategy for making it through baggage claim, when I spotted Daniel.

"Need a hand, lady?" he asked, grinning at me and holding out his arms for Zoe.

"I wasn't expecting you," I said.

"You gave me your itinerary. I thought that was a hint."

I kissed his cheek. "It wasn't, but I sure am glad to see you."

I transferred Zoe onto his shoulder.

She opened one eye briefly, gave Daniel a sleepy little smile, wrapped her legs around his waist and snuggled her head into the crook of his neck.

We retrieved my suitcase from baggage claim and stepped outside, to find Daniel's police car sitting smugly in a tow-away zone.

"There are some definite advantages to dating a cop," I said.

"I knew you'd learn to appreciate my finer qualities."

We settled Zoe into the back seat and headed for the 405 going north.

"Any news about Sara?" I asked.

"Still in a coma," Daniel said. "The doctors aren't predicting when, or if, she'll come to."

I felt a chill settle over me. I'd assumed that Sara was going to be all right. The thought that she might die, or end up some kind of vegetable, was intolerable. If the same person was responsible for both Sara and Wesley, we were going to solve this, whatever it took.

"I've got something interesting to tell you," Daniel said. "We had a breakthrough in the case tonight, thanks to you."

"Is that why you picked me up?"

"Nope, I picked you up because I missed you. We can finish playing detective in the morning."

"Don't keep me in suspense," I said. "What happened?"

"Remember that waiter you talked to at Spago, the one who'd seen Wesley with an attractive young lady?"

"I remember."

"He called us a few hours ago. It was his night off and he was watching a rerun of Friends. There was an actress in a bit part, whom he recognized as Wesley's girlfriend. We called the studio and got her name."

"Who?" I asked.

"Veronica Hayden."

I emitted a low whistle. No wonder she'd stood him up at Spago. She must have been driving there when she had the auto accident.

"I have to admire the role she played when we interviewed her," Daniel said. "She played the perfect upset patient. Completely appropriate for someone who was grateful to her doctor, but didn't know him very well."

"Have you talked to her yet?"

"I'm not that efficient. I thought I'd stop by and see her tomorrow."

Daniel pulled up in front of my condo and carried the still sleeping Zoe to her room. I took off her shoes and tucked her in, while he went back for the luggage.

I met him at the foot of the stairs.

"Oh, by the way," he said. "I almost forgot to tell you, we've got Eddie in custody."

"You're kidding," I said. "How?"

"Emilia stayed at your house over the weekend and we got lucky. He called on Friday night and we traced the call. It was coming from an extension at Memorial. Hospital security found the extension, and we nabbed him." Daniel looked inordinately pleased with himself.

"Who was he?"

"Name's Eddie Diaz. He's a maintenance man at Memorial. He's also a member of one of those fringe, Right-to-Life groups you love so much. You weren't the only doctor doing abortions, who was getting phone calls from Eddie."

"How was he getting the unlisted numbers? He had my back-line and my new number."

"From the listing in Labor and Delivery. You had to give them all your numbers."

I felt a shudder of fear, followed by fury. One of my fellow residents had gone into practice in the Midwest. She was the only person performing abortions in the southern half of her state, and used to tell me stories about how the Right-to-Lifers would picket her house and harass her children at school, telling them their mother was a murderer.

Here, in progressive Los Angeles, I'd thought myself safe from those right-wing quacks.

"Well, thanks," I said. "You've taken a big load off my mind. I was really starting to worry about those phone calls."

"You know, honey, there's nothing wrong with employing a professional. I wouldn't take out my own appendix. I'd call you. So, why catch your own pervert, if you've got me to do it for you?"

I laughed. "In exchange, I have Ellie Bennett's last known address. She and the orthopedist were divorced twelve years ago."

"Sounds like you had a successful trip to Connecticut."

"Actually, it was rather sad. Ben's mother has Alzheimer's. She doesn't remember that two of her four children are dead. Irving, Ben's father, is very old and frail. It made me want to cry, just seeing him."

"I'm sorry," Daniel said.

"I don't suppose you'd like to stay the night?" I asked.

He wrapped his arms around me, hard-muscled chest, a scent of fresh soap, gentle hands stroking my back and my buttocks. "It just so happens I packed my jammies, my shaver and a clean shirt in my gym bag."

"What a coincidence." I brushed his lips with my tongue, pulled him hard against me.

"You know," he said, "if we lived together, I wouldn't have to worry about whether I'd forgotten my pajamas."

I woke at about six-thirty, rolled over and noticed Daniel's bare back facing me. It was smooth, tanned, and muscular, the curve of the backbone inviting a trail of kisses. He hadn't needed his pajamas after all. I weighed the temptation against the probability of accomplishing anything amusing in the twenty minutes before Zoe woke up, and opted to let him sleep.

His suggestion about living together reverberated through my head. If I took him up on it, there'd be a lot more opportunity to indulge my baser instincts, not to mention, an adult across the table at dinner and someone with whom to split the interminable tasks of running a household. He could be a full-time friend, lover and ally—or a potential disaster in the making.

Just because Daniel was great in bed, fabulous during romantic vacations, and could deflect my obscene phone calls, didn't necessarily mean he'd hold up through the humdrum of daily living. If it weren't for Zoe, I'd consider taking my chances, but my responsibilities as a mother far outweighed any impulse I had to say yes.

"Planning a heart transplant?" Daniel rolled toward me and opened his eyes. "You look so serious."

I smiled at him. "Just thinking about last night."

"Are you deciding you're mad at me after all?"

I answered him with a kiss, slipping my hand under the blanket and caressing his warm thigh.

"I was thinking about living together. You took me by surprise."

He captured my hand, and put it somewhere more conducive to serious conversation. "I don't mean to rush you into anything you're not ready for. It's just easier for me to tell you, up front, what I'm thinking and feeling. I'm not very good at playing games and I wish you'd be honest with me."

His face was calm, serious and curious. The only thing that gave him away was a sudden tremor at the corner of his mouth.

I lifted a finger to the tremulous cheek.

"Daniel, I'm not one of those women who's afraid to make a commitment, or who distrusts men on principle. I was happily married for a long time, and I've never really been burned in a relationship. My main concern is Zoe. She's bonding to you. If you move in, you'll become her *de facto* daddy, the only one she's ever had, and if things between us don't work, I don't know what it might do to her. That's what's making me cautious."

"Not that you don't love me?"

I imagined what it had cost his pride to ask that question. I shook my head. "It's not that. I do love you. How could I not love someone who's been there for me so consistently?"

"And who's such a stud in bed. You forgot that part," he said.

I rolled over on top of him, and pinned him, laughing.

"Did it ever occur to you that Zoe's a major motive for both of us to make this work? I've always wanted to be someone's father. I never thought it would happen. The fact that you have Zoe makes you even more desirable," he said, kissing me.

I sighed, happy. "If I become any more desirable, Zoe is going to walk in here and find us doing something naughty."

I heard the sound of running water from down the hall.

Daniel reached to the side of the bed and retrieved his gym bag. "I knew there was a good reason I brought these pajamas."

CHAPTER THIRTY-SEVEN

I PHONED MY OFFICE AT EIGHT-THIRTY THAT morning, and left word with my secretary that I would be in that afternoon. I was glad that I always scheduled a patient-free catch-up day after a trip. That meant I didn't have to choose between seeing my patients, and tagging along with Daniel for what promised to be an interesting interview with Veronica Hayden. This had taken some persuasion on my part, but Daniel had given in. I guess he didn't want to risk ruining our reconciliation.

Veronica lived in south Beverly Hills, near Olympic, in an elderly but well-kept apartment building. Daniel had decided against calling first. No point in giving her an opportunity to rehearse her lines.

Daniel rang the bell and we waited while she scrutinized us through the peephole. The door opened a few inches, the chain still fastened.

"Miss Hayden, I'm Lieutenant Ross. I spoke with you in the hospital after your surgery. May we come in?"

I noticed Daniel didn't introduce me. I guess he wanted her to assume I was with the police.

"I know who you are, lieutenant. What do you want?"

"Just to talk with you for a minute. There are a few pieces of information I think you can help us with."

She closed the door and reopened it, ushering us into the darkened interior of her apartment. It appeared as if we'd woken her up. An unmade sofa-bed occupied one corner of the living room. The drapes were closed, and the only light was from a small, bedside lamp. Veronica was wearing a white terry-cloth robe and a pair of rubber thongs. A mass of disheveled black hair fell around her face. She pushed it back with both hands and stared at us, as if daring us to comment on the multiple, fine red scars that crisscrossed what had once been an extraordinary face. Even in the dark, the extent of the damage was impressive.

"Have a seat if you can find one," she said. "If you don't mind, I'd like to get dressed first."

She picked up a purse, which was lying on the coffee table, and disappeared down a small hallway.

I walked to the windows, pulled the blackout drapes and let sunlight flood the room. Apart from the unmade bed, it was neat and attractive, furnished with inexpensive, light woods and decorated with plants. Dramatic print fabrics, stretched onto wood frames, substituted for artwork, reminding me of my own student days. A 1940s kitchen, with old linoleum countertops, was scrubbed spotless. A small dining table with four wicker chairs provided the only seating alternative to the bed. I removed a few newspapers and sat down, waiting. I could hear the sound of running water and the buzz of an electric toothbrush.

Finally, Veronica emerged, wearing a form-fitting, long-sleeved, black T-shirt and jeans, as if showing off her spectacular figure could somehow compensate for the ravaged face. I noticed she'd put on make-up, and from a distance, the camouflage was almost perfect. Her dark hair was combed in bangs over her forehead and cut to fall across her cheeks. The skin under the make-up seemed smooth. Wesley had done a good job. Perhaps, after the redness faded, the scars wouldn't be noticeable. But, in the harsh glare of sunlight, the thickness of the foundation cream was obvious.

"I don't know what more I can tell you, lieutenant," she said, seating herself opposite us. "As you know, I was recovering from general anesthetic when Dr. Templeton was killed."

"Where were you going, the night of the accident, Miss Hayden?" Daniel asked.

She gave him a puzzled look. "I was on my way to meet a friend for dinner," she said.

"At Spago?"

She glanced down at the table, then raised her chin and stared straight at him. "Yes, at Spago."

"One of the waiters there recognized you as a frequent companion of Dr. Templeton's. Why didn't you tell us you knew him socially?" Daniel asked.

"I didn't think it was any of your business, lieutenant. I obviously didn't kill him, so what difference could it make that we were friends?"

"Friends? Or lovers?" he said.

"What do you think?"

"I think you were lovers. I also think you called him at seven-thirty, to give him an excuse to leave home and meet you for dinner."

"Is it a crime to have dinner with one's physician?" she asked, mouth tightening, hands toying with the pepper grinder on the table.

Daniel shook his head. "Of course not. But you can be

prosecuted for deliberately withholding vital evidence from the police in a murder investigation."

Her lower lip trembled, but she held her ground. "I don't see how my dinner plans have anything to do with the murder."

"How long had you been having an affair with Wesley Templeton?" he asked.

She shrugged. "A few months."

"Did you know he was married?"

"Of course, I did. I'm not a complete fool. I didn't expect him to leave his wife for me, or even to be around for very long. Wesley was charming, intelligent, generous, and not very happy with his wife. I had fun with him, and married or not, it was better than being alone. L.A. is a tough town for hopeful young actresses."

Daniel's voice was gentle. "I wouldn't imagine anyone, as attractive as you are, would have much trouble meeting people."

A tear trembled on her lower lid and rolled down her cheek. "I look just lovely now, don't I?"

I reached into my purse and handed her a tissue.

"You had a good plastic surgeon," I said softly. "From here, with make-up on, I can hardly see the scars. I'll bet, in a few months, they'll all fade."

"You think so?"

I nodded.

"Did Dr. Templeton's wife know about your relationship?" Daniel asked.

"I don't think so. Wesley told me he didn't want to hurt his wife. He was pretty careful. Always had an airtight excuse for not being home and never spent the night here."

"Did he have any enemies that you know about?"

She shook her head. "If I had the slightest idea who

killed him, I'd tell you. Honestly, I would. I cared for Wesley. I just don't know anything about his life that would help."

"All right, Miss Hayden. If I think of anything else, I'll be in touch."

"Lieutenant?"

Daniel paused in the act of getting out of his chair.

"Does Mrs. Templeton know about this?"

Daniel shook his head.

"Please, don't tell her. Wesley didn't want to hurt his wife and I don't either. She's obviously been through a lot in the past few weeks."

"I don't see any reason for this to go beyond the three of us, at the moment, Miss Hayden." Daniel got to his feet, and I followed him.

CHAPTER THIRTY-EIGHT

WE STEPPED OUTSIDE AND WALKED IN SILENCE, down the block to his car. The air was already promising a very warm day. The leaves on the jacaranda trees made a shadowed lattice on the sidewalk.

"I can't help feeling sorry for her," I said. "She reminds me of a kid in dress-up clothes, with all of her fantasies suddenly fallen apart."

"I know what you mean." Daniel massaged my neck with one hand. "Shall I drop you off at your office?"

I shook my head. "I think there's one more person we need to visit. I just had a stroke of genius."

We opened the car doors and settled ourselves inside.

I swiveled to face him and reached for my purse. "Ellie Bennett, Wesley's former mistress, divorced her husband twelve years ago. She remarried and left Connecticut. Her husband claimed that the two of them hadn't been in touch since his last child support payment, but I persuaded him to give me her new married name and last known address. I'd always assumed that Ellie was a nickname for Ellen or

Eleanor. Then I realized there was another possibility." I handed him the scrap of paper.

"Ellie Johnson, 3215 Bluebird Way, Bellevue," he read.

"Bellevue's a suburb of Seattle," I said. "And Ellie is a nickname for Helen. I'll bet you dinner at the most expensive restaurant in town that Ellie Bennett and Helen Johnson, the circulating nurse, are one and the same."

"Oh, come on. Johnson's a pretty common name," Daniel said. "I don't buy it. I can't imagine a narcissistic Beverly Hills plastic surgeon, who devotes his career to creating physical perfection, being involved with a woman who looks like Helen Johnson."

"Maybe she put on a little weight in twenty-one years," I said.

"It still doesn't make sense. But it's easy enough to check out."

He accelerated around a corner and headed for the station house. For a confirmation of my guess, we had to have a computer and a fax.

Forty-five minutes later, we had it. The personnel office at University Hospital in Seattle gave us Helen Johnson's home address on Bluebird Way, and the Washington State Department of Motor Vehicles faxed us a photo of Ellie Bennett's license.

Daniel toasted me with a cup of stale coffee. "Miss Marple scores another coup."

"Now, now," I said, with becoming modesty. "Just because she knew him, doesn't mean she killed him. Everyone seems to have been on intimate terms with the doctor."

A quick call to West Beverly revealed that Mrs. Johnson had worked the night before, and was scheduled to be on tonight as well. That made it a fair bet that she was sleeping at the moment, and a surprise afternoon visit was likely to find her at home.

The Johnsons lived in a sweet little neighborhood of post-war bungalows, tucked in a corner, south of Pico and east of Barrington. The houses were all one story, no more than a thousand square feet, and neatly painted. Quite a number of them had charming Japanese gardens. There was a single Ford Escort parked in the driveway of the Johnson home. We pulled up behind it and rang the bell.

We kept ringing for a good five minutes before Helen came to the door. It was clear we'd awakened her, and she was none too pleased about it.

"Detective?" She yawned widely and covered her mouth with plump white fingers. "What is it?"

The door remained only half open, her huge bulk, in a voluminous, baby-blue housecoat, blocking our entry.

"Sorry to wake you, Mrs. Johnson. We need your help. Can we come in for a few minutes?"

She shrugged, as though there was no point in refusing, since we'd already ruined her sleep, and motioned us to follow her inside.

The living room was small and dark, even at mid-day. Helen turned on a pair of matching ginger jar lamps, on either side of a chintz sofa, and seated herself opposite it, in a large leather recliner. The coffee table was imitation Italian provincial and covered with cut glass knickknacks. The side table contained a wedding photo of Mr. and Mrs.

Johnson. The bride hadn't been noticeably thinner on her wedding day. The groom could be described as portly, and had a round, amiable face with a small mustache.

"I think I've already told you everything I can remember, lieutenant," she said.

"I think not," Daniel said. "You neglected to tell us that your previous name was Helen Bennett, known as Ellie to your friends."

Helen stared at him, saying nothing.

Daniel let the silence grow for a while, and then continued. "Eighteen years ago, Wesley Templeton had an affair with a woman named Ellie Bennett, an affair that produced an illegitimate child. Your child, Mrs. Johnson. I think that information is very relevant, don't you?"

"That's a fascinating supposition, assuming you can prove it. Do I look like the kind of woman men find irresistible?" she asked.

I tried to imagine Wesley making passionate love to her. If I hadn't seen the evidence in writing, I'd have dismissed the idea as ridiculous.

"Wesley saved all your letters, Mrs. Johnson. They're very explicit, and they speak for themselves. Does your daughter know who her father is?"

She seemed to cave inward, as if someone had opened a valve and let out the air. I had a sudden vision of her mounds of flesh collapsing into a puddle on the floor.

"No," she whispered. "Valerie has no idea."

"And there's no reason for her to find out," I said. "We're not here to hurt anyone or destroy any families. We just need all the information we can get about Dr. Templeton. Why don't you tell us what you know?"

Helen sat straight in her chair, composing herself with what appeared to be some effort.

"If you read my letters, you know that Wesley and I parted as friends. I haven't seen or heard from him since a few months after Valerie was born."

"He was the father of your child," Daniel said. "You mean to tell me, that in all this time, you were never tempted to pick up the phone and talk to him, tell him how Valerie was doing?"

She shook her head. "Do you have children, lieutenant?"

"No."

"Once you have a child, that child's well-being becomes the most important priority in your life. Valerie loves the man who raised her, my former husband Gordon. He was, and still is, an excellent father. The last thing in the world I wanted was for Wesley to come back into our lives and disrupt our family. I was grateful that he was willing to leave Valerie to me and not interfere."

"Yet, your family was disrupted," Daniel said. "You and your first husband split up. Did he know about Valerie? Is that why you were divorced?"

"No, he never knew. We divorced because we grew apart, like a lot of couples. But he was always fair and responsible, and he was always there for Valerie, even after we separated."

"Did Templeton's wife know you and he had an affair?"

"Not while we were together," Helen said. "They weren't married then. I don't know if she found out afterwards or not. Did they stay married?"

Daniel shook his head. "They were divorced. A hit-and-run driver struck Sara Templeton just a few days ago. She's in a coma. We don't know if she'll live."

Helen's expression didn't change. "I'm sorry to hear that," she said.

"Did you contact Dr. Templeton after you moved to Los Angeles?" Daniel asked.

"I had no idea he lived in Los Angeles. I was astounded when I saw him walk into the operating suite at West Beverly."

"He must have been equally astounded to see you," Daniel said.

"Not at all. Wesley didn't recognize me. When we were lovers, twenty years ago, I weighed one- hundred-and-twenty pounds and was a brunette. I don't suppose I can blame him for not making the connection."

"You must have been hurt," he said. "And angry."

"I was immensely relieved," she said. "Look, I'm happily married to a very nice man. My child is a healthy, well-adjusted young woman. The last thing I need in my life is an ex-lover I stopped caring about years ago. All I wanted was to finish the case, stay out of Wesley's way, and go home before he had any opportunity to jog his memory."

"No danger of that now, is there?" Daniel said. "You don't ever have to worry about Wesley entering your life again."

"What are you implying? That I killed him?"

"Did you?"

Helen rose from her chair, looming large and formidable across the coffee table. "I managed to avoid Wesley Templeton for eighteen years without resorting to murder, lieutenant. I assure you, I had no reason to kill him. If you have any further questions for me, you can ask them in front of my attorney. Please go, now."

We went. Daniel backed his car out of the driveway and headed north, in the direction of the station.

"There is no physical evidence linking her to the murder," Daniel said.

"Do you think she did it?" I asked.

"I don't know. Everything she said made sense to me, assuming it's true that he didn't recognize her."

"I'd believe that part," I said. "But I find it hard to believe she wasn't hurt and insulted, that a man she had a child with, didn't even know who she was."

"She may have been hurt, but I can also believe that she considered it a lucky break." Daniel reached for his police radio. "Anything I need to know before I head back to the station?" he asked the dispatcher.

I saw him nod, grin and make a right turn at the next corner.

"Good news," he said. "Sara's regained consciousness. How about a visit to Memorial?"

CHAPTER THIRTY-NINE

"GOD, AM I GLAD TO SEE YOU AWAKE." I WAS grinning like an idiot, holding Sara's hand.

She looked only marginally more alive than when I'd last seen her, although most of the tubes were gone and they'd transferred her out of intensive care to a large cheerful room, with a view of the mountains and a television.

She managed a weak smile. "I don't suppose you brought me a peanut butter sandwich?"

"As soon as they let you eat, I'll bring you take out from the best restaurant in town," I promised. "How do you feel?"

"Like I was run over by a Mack truck," she said. "Do you know what happened? The last thing I remember is paying for some groceries on a check-out line."

"Hit and run," I said.

No point in telling her we suspected attempted murder. That could wait a while.

"The docs said they fixed everything that was broken. You'll be fine in a few weeks."

"I'm glad you're here." She squeezed my hand, and I held hers tighter.

"I went to your apartment, while you were in the hospital," I said. "I brought a nightgown and a few toilet articles for you. Is there anything else you'd like?"

"A hot bath, but I suppose that's out of the question."

"Sara, can you remember anything that happened the night of the accident? When I was in your apartment, I noticed a suitcase. It looked as if you'd been out of town."

Sara nodded slowly. "I was on a quest. I wanted to meet Wesley's daughter."

"Valerie? Why? Why now?"

"Because it's time for me to move on with my life, and Valerie is a loose end. I wanted to talk to her mother, see if I could validate everything I assumed about Wesley's behavior. And I needed to see what Valerie looked like. I wouldn't have told her who I was, or who Wesley was. She's an innocent bystander. I just wanted to see her."

"And did you?"

Sara nodded again, letting go of my hand and pressing her fingers against her forehead, as if she were trying to retrieve images buried in the fog of her coma.

"It wasn't that difficult. Ellie, Wesley's mistress had been married to a doctor, and doctors are always listed somewhere. He was practicing in Connecticut. I went to see him, pretended to be an old friend of hers, and asked for her home number. He was very pleasant at first, told me they'd been divorced for years and she'd remarried. That was when I made my mistake. I assumed he was probably angry with her, and I thought I could make him an ally, so I told him the truth, who I was, and that my husband had been involved with his ex-wife, years ago. I didn't say anything about Valerie. I didn't know if Ellie had ever confessed to him."

"How did he react?"

"He shut down completely. He said that he was certain Ellie would have no interest in speaking to me, or in becoming involved in my nasty divorce over an incident that was ancient history in her life. He refused to give me her address."

"So, how did you get it?"

"I didn't. But I got Valerie's. His nurse called him out of the room for a minute. There was some problem with one of his patients. He left his cell phone on his desk. While he was out, I skimmed through his contacts. You want to hear something funny? Valerie lives in Los Angeles. I flew three thousand miles to find someone who lives fifteen minutes away."

"Is that where you were, the night you had this accident, visiting Valerie?"

Sara began to say something that was interrupted by a deep, hacking cough.

I helped her turn to her side and offered her a glass of water.

She took a few sips, breathed a harsh, raspy sound and continued. "*Visiting* is something of an exaggeration. I went to her apartment and rang the bell. She opened the door with the chain on the latch. I only caught a brief glimpse of her, but there's no question she's Wesley's daughter. She has his hair, his eyes, even that same little birthmark at the corner of her mouth. Pretty girl, too much make-up. If the bastard hadn't sterilized himself and not bothered to tell me, I could have had one just like her."

"What did you say to her?"

"I said that my name was Sara, that I'd known her

mother years ago, and I wanted to talk to her for a few minutes. She asked me to wait. I heard voices, as if she were consulting with someone, then she came back to the door and said she was sorry, she couldn't let me in. So, I left and went grocery shopping. That's all I remember."

"Do you remember her address?" I asked.

Sara shook her head.

It was obvious the whole conversation was a major effort for her.

"It's probably still in my car," she said. "Where is my car? Did you drive it home?"

I hadn't.

"It's probably still sitting where you parked it," I said. "Do you remember where that is?"

Sara shook her head and winced. "Probably at the grocery store."

"I'll find it. I'll take the keys and put it in your garage for you. When you're feeling a little better, I'll bring you your mail and anything else you need from your house."

I bent down and kissed her forehead. She smelled of talcum powder and hospital mouthwash. I was incredibly glad to see her.

"I'll be back tomorrow," I said.

Daniel was waiting for me in the hospital cafeteria, chewing on a muffin and drinking a cup of coffee. Something Andrea had said kept reverberating in my head.

"No one seems to have a motive," I'd told her.

"Maybe something happened that night that created a motive," she'd answered.

One very important thing had happened that night. Veronica Hayden had been in a car crash, a hit-and-run. We'd all assumed her accident had been only coincidentally related to Wesley's subsequent death. Had it, instead, been a botched murder attempt? Could someone have wanted to kill Wesley, his current mistress and his ex-wife? Put that way, Erica seemed the most likely candidate, but she had an airtight alibi for the questionable suicide of Josie Otero. I ran my hand through my hair, pulling it in frustration, as solutions touched the periphery of my consciousness and eluded it.

"How is she?" Daniel asked.

I appreciated his tact in allowing me to see Sara alone. "Awake and talking. You'll never guess where she was the night of the accident. She tracked down Valerie Bennett. It turns out that Valerie lives in Los Angeles, not far from here. Sara went to see her."

"Did she tell her about Wesley?"

I shook my head. "Apparently, not. First of all, Valerie wouldn't let her in the house, and secondly, Sara is a nice woman. It wasn't Valerie's fault that her mother had an affair with Sara's husband. I don't think Sara would intentionally turn Valerie's life upside-down."

Daniel tossed his empty coffee cup into the trash and headed for the nearest phone. Information had no listing for a Valerie Bennett.

"You don't suppose she lives with her mother, do you?" he asked.

"I doubt it. Sara said the address was in her car. It's probably still in the grocery store lot."

Daniel shook his head. "It's been more than a week. It probably got towed. Do you know what make it is?"

"Volvo, dark blue sedan."

I waited, watching young doctors in scrubs and hospital employees snacking on fried chicken and frozen yogurt, while Daniel phoned his office.

"It's in the Culver City tow yard," Daniel said. "I had the sergeant call them and release the car to us, no charge."

"You're a prince," I said.

We headed for the parking lot. I was jumpy and agitated, and I wasn't sure why. We were getting close. All my instincts said so, and I felt afraid. I just wished I had some way of predicting what the killer's next move was going to be.

The police tow yard was in a grimy, industrial section of Culver City. I was glad it was still light out and that I was driving through the neighborhood with an armed police-man. We went inside, and I waited while Daniel exhibited his ID, and talked to the police clerk at the desk. We followed him out to the back lot and he presented us with Sara's filthy car. I handed Daniel the keys, and drew my finger along the grime on the hood, promising myself to give it a wash before depositing it in Sara's pristine garage.

Daniel opened the passenger door and checked through the glove compartment. I started on the driver's side, and finally found the crumpled piece of paper I was seeking on the floor. I smoothed it out and read the address.

The pieces fell into place. It was as if I'd been looking at one of those Escher prints, one picture in black on white, and an entirely different one when you blink your eyes, refocus your brain and view it as white on black. Andrea had been right. Something had happened that night to create a compelling motive for murder. And I knew, beyond a shadow of a doubt, who had committed it. I also had a very good idea of what the killer's next move had to be.

CHAPTER FORTY

"**C**AN'T YOU DRIVE ANY FASTER?" I ASKED DANIEL. "Not without a siren or having an accident."

The car sped up La Cienega in the direction of Memorial. It was late afternoon and rush hour. Commuters headed south in the direction of the freeway. Shoppers poured out of the Beverly Center scattering for home. The left turn at Third Street seemed to take an hour.

"If anything else happens to Sara, I'll never forgive myself."

"Calm down. I've got a police guard at the nurses station, making sure she gets no visitors."

The police radio signaled and Daniel acknowledged.

Sergeant Jordan's voice came through. "No luck, boss. We surrounded the suspect's house, but no one's home. I'm going to leave two guys there, in case anyone returns, and head over to West Beverly. Maybe we'll have better luck there."

"Acknowledged," Daniel said. "We're pulling into the parking lot at Memorial. We'll make sure Sara Hellman is safe, tell her what we suspect, double her security and join you."

We parked in the doctor's lot on the mezzanine and found the elevators. It took forever for one to come. Sara's new room was on the orthopedic floor, and a hospital security guard was stationed at a pair of double doors leading to the nursing station. He was passing out visitor badges labeled with the visitor's name and the room number of the patient being visited. The LAPD guard was seated close by.

"Everything's quiet, sir," he said, recognizing Daniel. "There haven't been any visitors for Miss Hellman all day. She's resting quietly."

I breathed a sigh of relief, and preceded Daniel down the corridor. At the far end, a familiar figure in a nurse's uniform, carrying a dinner tray, entered Sara's room.

I was hit by the same thought I had, when I had visited Sara in the ICU. People in hospital uniforms are invisible. Put on scrubs and a stethoscope, or a nurse's whites, and you could go anywhere without being challenged.

Daniel spotted her at the same moment I did, and we both began to run.

She was bending over Sara, handing her a glass of apple juice.

"Don't drink that," I said to Sara, as Daniel grabbed the nurse and pinned her arms behind her back.

She struggled for a minute, but she was no match for a cop who could bench-press a hundred and fifty pounds.

"What's going on?" Sara looked at us, scared and bewildered.

I took the drink from her hand and replaced it on the tray.

"One of these clear liquids is likely to be lethal to you," I said. "We need to save the meal for our forensic science department. Let me introduce you to the person who was responsible for your hit-and-run accident. Sara Hellman, meet Helen Johnson, formerly Ellie Bennett."

"You're Ellie?" Sara asked, shocked.

Helen shrugged her shoulders. Her huge bosom heaved with the effort. "Not what you expected, am I?"

"But, why?" Sara asked. "Why would you want to kill me, after all these years? What did I ever do to you? You're the one who had the affair with my husband, the woman who had the child he refused to have with me."

Helen was silent.

"It's more complicated than that, Sara," I said. "It has to do with Valerie. You needed to see her for your own peace of mind and you traced her. I suspect Gordon Bennett told Ellie you had been to Connecticut, and the one thing Ellie never wanted her daughter to know was that Wesley was her father."

"But I wouldn't have told her," Sara said. She turned to Helen. "Truly, I wouldn't have done that. I had no reason to hurt Valerie."

"Helen had no way of knowing that," I said. "And even if she had, it wouldn't have mattered. The risk you posed was too great. Helen must have been at Valerie's apartment that night. She followed you when you left, and ran you over at the first opportunity. If you hadn't left your car, she would probably have found another way to kill you."

I turned to Helen. "You thought that Sara was the only person who could make the final connection, the missing piece of knowledge that you had to keep from Valerie at all costs. When I saw Valerie's address it all made sense. Valerie moved to Los Angeles a year ago to become an actress. She changed her name to something with more Hollywood pizzazz—Veronica Hayden. As Veronica, she met and had an affair with a married plastic surgeon, old enough to be her father."

"Wesley," Sara whispered. Then she started to laugh and cry all at the same time. "Just as I think I've uncovered every despicable thing Wesley's ever done, I discover something else—incest with his own illegitimate daughter. You must have wanted to kill him."

"I did kill him," Helen said, finally breaking the silence. "I didn't want to, but I couldn't see any other way."

"Before you say anything else," Daniel said, "I have to read you your rights. You have the right to remain silent and you may ask for an attorney at any time. Anything you say now can be used against you in a court of law."

"It doesn't matter." Daniel let go of her arms and she slid into an armchair at the foot of the bed.

Daniel removed a small digital recorder from a case on his belt. "When did you learn they were having an affair?" he asked gently.

"The night I killed Wesley. Valerie had been over that afternoon. I asked her to stay for dinner, but she said she had a date with a man she'd been seeing for the past six months. I asked her if it was anyone she was serious about, anyone she'd like us to meet but she said no. He was a married plastic surgeon, about to separate from his wife and she didn't think he was husband material.

"Then she told me his name. I was horrified and I didn't know what to do. I had no idea Wesley was even living in Los Angeles. How can you tell your daughter that the man she'd grown up loving as her father wasn't, and the man she was screwing was? I was beside myself. Then I got a call to come in and circulate for an emergency at West Beverly.

"After that the nightmare got even more macabre. Wesley Templeton walked into the operating room and when they wheeled the patient in, it was Valerie. My beautiful baby, with her gorgeous face in shreds, because she'd been driving to meet her father, her lover.

"I was frantic. I couldn't tell Valerie the truth. And if I told Wesley, asked him to get out of her life, I couldn't be certain he wouldn't tell her. Killing him seemed to be the only way."

Sara was listening, mesmerized by the story, nodding as though the conclusion was completely logical. I almost expected her to applaud. I wondered if a jury hearing Helen would be as moved to tears as Sara was.

"During the surgery, I slipped a vial of medication and a syringe out of Dr. Venning's anesthesia cart. When they sent me out of the room to get more suture, I filled it and slipped it in my pocket. I knew Wesley would be alone in the men's locker room, so I went in and waited in one of the bathroom stalls. I heard him come in, saw him bend down to get his shoes, and I grabbed him. I'm not very strong but I am very heavy. I sat on him and injected him. It only took a minute. Then I left the room and went home."

"And Josie Otero?" Daniel asked.

Helen shook her head. "I didn't want to kill Josie. I liked her. But she saw me leave the hospital when she was in her car, in the parking lot. I was supposed to have left before her. I don't think she wanted to believe the implications of what she'd seen, so she invited me over, to see if I had some plausible explanation. I still had an old vial of sleeping pills. I always kept my old prescriptions. You never know when you'll need them again, and worst case, their efficacy may be a little less. When she went to the kitchen to get us some cookies, I dissolved them all in her tea."

She started to cry, great sobs that shook her breasts and belly. Slowly she raised herself out of the chair. "And I did it all for nothing. There'll be a trial now and Valerie will find out all about it anyway. Her name, and mine, will be all over the media. Her life will be destroyed."

"One more question," Daniel said. "How were you going to kill Sara? What did you put in her food?"

Helen started to laugh. "Nothing," she said. "I didn't put anything in her food. I was going to kill her with this."

She pulled a small revolver from the pocket of her uniform.

Daniel started to move.

"Don't," Helen said.

She grabbed me with one arm and pressed the revolver to the base of my neck. The metal was a cool, terrifying circle. My muscles began an involuntary tremor and I heard the pounding of my heart doing double time. *Please no. I don't want to die. Don't, Helen. God, please don't.*

"Helen, killing us all won't change anything. There are others who know that you killed Wesley. Don't make things worse for yourself," Daniel said, quietly, calmly.

She gripped me more tightly. I couldn't see her face, only Daniel's, looking at me with love and with terror.

"There can't be a trial," she said. "And Valerie mustn't find out the truth. Promise me."

"I promise," Daniel said.

The sound of the gunshot reverberated through my head, along with Sara's scream. The arm around me loosened, and I felt Helen drop to the floor. And then, as everything started to spin, I felt Daniel holding me up, touching me, whispering over and over, "My love."

EPILOGUE

Zoe was writing a story. Her little face was screwed up in concentration. Her knuckles turned white as she gripped the pencil and carefully formed a large letter B.

I looked at her mass of curly brown hair, the sweetness of her smile, the tender young skin, and I knew that I would kill to protect her, or die for her, if necessary.

The mother of one of her kindergarten classmates had summed it up nicely. "I'd jump in front of a truck to save my kid," she'd said. "I can't say I'd do as much for my husband."

I understood Helen Johnson, and multiple murderer that she was, my heart ached for her. In the moments before the security staff reached the room, Daniel, Sara and I had all looked at one another and silently promised to do all that we could to protect Helen's secret.

A depressed nurse had killed herself in a patient's room, the newspaper had reported in a page two story in the Extra section. We left Josie's murder as a suicide, and Sara's hit-and-run attracted no attention. Wesley's murder would remain on the books as one of the many unsolved crimes in the big city.

Sara was getting out of the hospital after six weeks in rehabilitation. They'd removed the cast yesterday. I'd had her place cleaned and brought over the fixings for a *Welcome Home* lunch. Daniel and I planned to drive over to Memorial to pick her up and then cook it together.

In the meantime, Zoe and I were expected at Daniel's place for breakfast. I ran a comb through her tangled curls and slipped my purse over my shoulder.

Daniel's cottage looked bright and welcome in the summer sunshine. The white paint sparkled. Zinnias lined the walkway.

"Hi, Princess." He opened the door, scooped up Zoe and gave her a kiss. "You ready to make the eggs?"

"Yup, yup, yup," she said, heading for the kitchen.

"Hello, love." He kissed me lightly on the lips, tilting my chin up with one finger. "Make yourself comfortable. The cooks will tell you when breakfast is ready."

I walked through the living room, running my hand over the cool leather of the sofa we'd made love on the very first time, admiring his few good pieces of southwest art. His bedroom was spare and neat, a double bed with a Navajo blanket, a pine chest, and a few photos. The closet door was open and I noticed a canvas suitcase tucked into a corner.

I lifted it out and opened it onto his bed. The inside seemed roomy, large enough for what I had in mind.

I turned to his dresser and began emptying the drawers one by one.

"Breakfast's ready." Daniel came into the room, stood behind me and slipped his arms around my waist.

I smiled.

"Are we going somewhere I don't know about?" he whispered into my hair.

"My house," I said. "Zoe and I got tired of hearing you complain all the time about packing your gym bag. This way, I promise, you'll never run out of pajamas."

ACKNOWLEDGMENTS

Many thanks to Linda Schreyer, my terrific editor, who helped make this novel so much better. Uri, my husband and technology guru read the drafts and kept my computer functioning. Thanks for being so much more adept at the more arcane aspects of Word than I am.

AUTHOR BIO

PAULA BERNSTEIN is a physician, a scientist, and the author of the Hannah Kline Mystery Series. Like her main character, Paula has spent her professional career as a practicing obstetrician gynecologist. In addition to her medical mystery series, her short story, *On Call for Murder,* was published in *LAst Resort,* the 2017 Sisters in Crime Anthology. Her website is www.HannahKlineMysteries.com.